ST. JOHN'S LUTHERAN
ELEMENTARY SCHOOL
"For a Christ-Centered Education"
3521 Linda Vista Ave.
Napa, California

Books by Larry Callen

The Muskrat War

The Muskrat War

• LARRY CALLEN •

An Atlantic Monthly Press Book
Little, Brown and Company   Boston/Toronto

FIRST EDITION

Library of Congress Cataloging in Publication Data

Callen, Larry.
  The muskrat war.

  "An Atlantic Monthly Press book."
  SUMMARY: Tough times in Four Corners get even
tougher when a group of swindlers comes to town.
  [1. Swindlers and swindling — Fiction. 2. Humorous
stories] I. Title.
PZ7.C134Mu   [Fic]   80-36700
ISBN 0-316-12498-2

ATLANTIC—LITTLE, BROWN BOOKS
ARE PUBLISHED BY
LITTLE, BROWN AND COMPANY
IN ASSOCIATION WITH
THE ATLANTIC MONTHLY PRESS

BP

Published simultaneously in Canada
by Little, Brown & Company (Canada) Limited

PRINTED IN THE UNITED STATES OF AMERICA

To a bunch of Callens
Willa, Erin, Alex, Dashiel, Holly,
Emily, Lawrence, Dorothy, David, Ann and Toni

and to nieces, nephews, and stuff

Alphonse Adam Autin, Jr.
Amelia Anne Autin
Diana Marie Autin
John Leonard Autin
Danielle Margaret Callen
Darryl Mark Callen
David Michael Callen
Elizabeth Padgett DiMaggio
Deborah Callen Feemster
Donna Callen Guidry
Peggy Autin Haschle
Denise Callen Middleton
Carol Alexis Padgett
Julianna Dorothy Padgett

Mimi Padgett
Patricia Maureen Padgett
Henry Joseph Sauviac IV
Lauren Marie Sauviac
Michael Callen Sauviac
Peter Slie
Betsy Kathleen Woods
Eugene Templeton
    Woods III
Jill Margaret Woods
Kenneth Paul Woods
Peggy Eileen Woods
Roy Patrick Woods
Sally Meredith Woods

Contents

The Muskrat War

◉ 1 ◉

Chicken Stealing

There's a chicken stealer loose in Four Corners. At first we thought it was some animal sneaking in our yard at night and killing a chicken and dragging it off somewhere. But there wasn't a drop of blood or a single loose feather on the ground.

"Things are getting pretty bad when one man's got to steal another man's chickens to get food on his table," Dad said. "Pinch, get some empty tin cans. Put rocks in them and string them to the gate and around the wire fence. If the chicken stealers come back, maybe we'll hear them."

He emptied the pellets out of two shotgun shells and filled them with rock salt. The sting would make those chicken stealers think long and hard about even looking sidewise at our chickens again. And they wouldn't be doing their thinking sitting down.

I didn't see Dad again until suppertime. Mom brought glasses of water to the table and sat down. Nobody talked. Then Dad broke the silence.

"I spent the whole day looking for work in the city. Why, it's even worse there than it is here."

He went back to his eating. Suddenly he turned to me.

"Son, has Charley's dad been doing any trapping?" Charley Riedlinger is a pretty good friend of mine.

"I don't know."

"I was told he might be." He did some chewing. "You know, Ben Riedlinger don't normally trap at all." He chewed a little more. "That man ain't got no right to trap around here. I been trapping that swampland for twenty years. And my paw before me. Nobody's got a right to another man's trapping land."

"I suppose they are hungry, same as us," Mom said.

He put his fork down on the table, took a piece of bread and started mopping up the gravy on his plate.

"That ain't got nothing to do with it. That don't give him any rights he didn't have before."

I figured I would finish off the meal with some bread and syrup while they talked, but when I reached for the bread it was all gone.

"Can I have another piece of bread?"

"Not till tomorrow," Mom said.

"How come?"

"You want to eat your share now and not have bread tomorrow?"

"Why can't I have it both times?"

Dad had finished wiping up the gravy and he chewed on the bread. He did it slow, like it wasn't tasting as good as usual. He swallowed and looked at me.

"I'm getting less in my traps, Pinch. That means less money coming in. That means less flour. That means less bread."

He wiped his mouth on his sleeve.

"I wish you two would stop talking about wanting another piece of bread while I'm chewing on my last mouthful." He looked at Mom. "Victoria, I took two pieces of bread. That's all I took. I just ate a little slower than Pinch."

"Will Grimball, you got a right to more bread than Pinch and me. You are the one who does the hard work." Mom stood up and started to clean the dishes off the table.

Dad smacked his fist down on the table hard enough to make the dish jump.

"Victoria, I only had two pieces of bread! What kind of man is going to take more than his share and watch his kin go hungry?" He snatched up his plate and carried it over to the sink. He didn't come back and help Mom and me clean off the table like he does most times. Instead, he opened the back door and went outside. The door slammed with a hollow sound.

I sat still and looked at the door. I was waiting for him to come back inside and maybe grin at me and Mom and then help with the dishes. But he didn't do it.

I turned to Mom, not asking, just looking. She picked up the gravy bowl. "Maybe you ought to go see if you can help, Pinch. He's probably out back boiling the new muskrat traps to get the oil off them."

Charley Riedlinger was waiting for me when I got outside.

"Can't play, Charley."

"I don't care," he said and started walking toward the road.

"Charley?"

"What?"

"Your paw been trapping?"

"Some."

"My dad says it's his land for trapping. He doesn't own it. But it's his for trapping."

"Pinch, he let you and me and Mr. John Barrow trap on it!"

"But not grown-ups."

"Well, it ain't your dad's land anyway. It's railroad land."

"Owning land and trapping on land is two different things. My grandpa trapped on that land."

"My dad says your dad doesn't own that land and he doesn't own those muskrats either. They belong to whoever catches them."

"Who you yelling at!"

"Who *you* yelling at!"

"You want to fight?"

"*You* want to fight?"

"Yeah!" I told him.

"Pinch!" Dad called from the backyard.

I turned to see what he wanted. He had a wood fire going under the iron pot he used to clean the traps. There were about two dozen new, shiny steel ones on the ground. He picked one up, pried the jaws open with his strong fingers, and shoved an iron nail between the teeth so the boiling water could clean them thorough. Then he dropped the trap in the water.

When I turned back to Charley, he was heading up the road for home. I hadn't planned on fussing with him and I don't think he planned on fussing with me. It just happened.

I walked to where Dad was working. He turned and saw me standing there, watching.

"You want to help, Pinch?" He turned back to the iron pot. The water was starting to steam.

"Pinch," Dad said, talking to me but not looking at me, "you are my favorite and only son. I don't want to pass on my troubles to you. We won't starve this winter, I promise you that. I'm putting out more traps. Your goat Loretta will have her kids pretty soon and the milk'll start and she'll be paying her way." When he leaned over to pick up more traps, I did too.

"Pinch, you got a whole pile of muskrat furs stored in the drying shed. Soon as you get a wagonload, we'll haul 'em to where I'm keeping mine in Judge

Ridley Boudreaux's barn. You did some pretty good trapping and I'm proud of you. That extra money is going to get us through the winter." He dropped another trap in the water.

"You know what I been figuring, Pinch?" He didn't wait for an answer. "The Judge has more goats he wants to sell. If we used the extra money to buy some, we'd really be in the goat-milk business. But I better go see him in the morning. I sure don't want him selling those goats to somebody else." He stopped his work and looked at me.

"You're a good son, Pinch," he said, smiling. "I don't think we'd of made it without your help." His big smile put a bigger smile on me.

◉ 2 ◉

Dog Meat

When Dad went inside to wash up, I paid a visit to Mr. Tony Carmouche. His grocery is right across the road.

"Mom says she needs turnips for soup," I told him. I was hoping he would be all out 'cause turnips in soup is like catsup on ice cream. But he found a couple.

"You hear about the chicken stealing?" I asked him.

"I did," he said, "and that ain't all that's going on. Times are bad. All kinds of things been happening around here lately. Even got to lock my doors. Never had to do that before. You know, a man came in the store yesterday and tried to sell me a case of medicine he said would put hair on a bald man's head. Looked and smelled just like mint tea. I told him there wasn't a single bald head in Four Corners, and he said it was good for getting rid of wrinkles and did we have any of them? I chased him out the store."

"Charley been around here?" I asked him.

"Not today, Pinch." He was trying to heft a box of canned beans from the floor to the counter, and it was almost too much for him. He is kind of a wiry man, with not too much muscle for lifting. I went over to give him a hand.

"Charley and me had a fuss," I told him.

"What about this time?"

"I don't know. He's got a head harder than my goat Loretta."

"Most boys got pretty hard heads. Nothing wrong with a head that's hard on the outside. It's when it hardens all the way through you got a problem." He stacked a few cans on the shelf. "If you ain't mad at him, best thing to do is go tell him. Maybe his head will soften and then both of you'll forget all about whatever's bothering you." He reached for more cans.

"Pinch, you know what's even harder than not getting angry when somebody is angry at you?"

"What?"

"Kissing a chicken on the lips."

"What?"

"You heard right, Pinch."

"Well, then, why is that?"

"Mainly, son, 'cause chickens don't have lips."

He was smiling. Maybe it was supposed to be funny.

Just then Mrs. Nell Carmouche, who is Mr. Tony's wife, walked into the store from the living quarters in back. She headed for the front door, walking birdy-legged and fast, like always. She nodded to me.

"Going to pay a visit to Pinch's mother," she told Mr. Tony. She is a lady who knows everything there is to know about how to hold a teacup. She helps my mom fix up the house every chance she gets, even when Mom isn't too keen on her helping.

"I'm leaving, too, Mr. Tony. Maybe I'll go see Charley, like you said." Truth is, I didn't want to stay around and listen to any more of his dumb jokes.

Mrs. Nell was halfway across the road by the time I got out on the porch. That's when the yelling started.

"Nell! You wait right there!"

It was Mr. John Barrow shouting. He was hurrying up the road on his long, skinny legs, waving his arms for her to stop.

"I got something to say to you," he yelled.

Mrs. Nell stood perfectly still and stared. She doesn't take to Mr. John Barrow, and sometimes there is fireworks when they meet. Her brow was furrowed and though I couldn't see her eyes, I knew they were shooting little pointy needles.

"You know what happened to my chickens?" Mr. John Barrow wasn't just asking her. He was shouting at her. She stared back.

"Something got to 'em, that's what," he shouted. "Your no-count hound been running around, chomping people's chickens again?"

She dropped her eyes to the road. Then she folded her hands together and looked straight at him again. The anger was gone. At least I couldn't see any. Only sadness.

"John, it couldn't be our dog. That dog died just last week."

Mr. Barrow took off his flappy hat and scratched his head.

"Well, I guess I'm sorry to hear it. Didn't take to him much, but nobody likes to hear about a dog dying."

"That's all right, John. He kind of did us a favor. He was old. Everything's got to go sometime. Besides, he timed it just right. Fresh meat's short at the store, so we been selling him to our customers, piece by piece."

Suddenly her eyes flashed up and fixed on Mr. John Barrow.

"You buy any fresh meat at the store this week, John?"

She held him in her stare. Then her eyes shifted. She continued across the road toward my house.

It took about a minute for Mr. John Barrow's face to settle back to its normal craftiness. He looked around and saw I was watching.

"She almost got me that time, Pinch," he said, kind of grinning. " 'Course, I knew she was joshing, but she almost got me. You knew she was joshing too, didn't you, Pinch? Tony would never sell dog meat at his store."

He stood there, waiting for me to say something. I just let him wait.

"Pinch, you know what happened to my chickens?"

"No."

"Something got to one of 'em, Pinch. And I didn't hear a thing. There should've been plenty of racket, but I didn't hear one squawk. Kind of like a ghost crept into the yard."

He decided to go inside the store and tell Mr. Tony. But Mr. Tony wouldn't let Mr. John Barrow get two cents in about chickens before he got in about a dollar's worth on who owed who for a month of groceries.

"Well, Tony, sorry you feel that way about it. I'll pay you when I can. But I don't like people yelling at me, I tell you that. And I'd change stores in a minute if there was another store to change to."

"John, I ain't exactly what you would call a big

man, but you lower your voice when you are in my store or I'll rap you hard in the mouth."

There was a silence. Then Mr. John Barrow gave Mr. Tony a little grin. Mr. Tony kept a serious look on his face until the grin got wider. Then he started grinning back just a little bit. Mr. John Barrow isn't much of a man for fighting.

About then Mrs. Nell came back in the store. She gave Mr. John Barrow a little nod, serious-faced, and walked into the back room.

"Tony, you got any fresh meat in the store?" Mr. John Barrow asked as soon as she was gone.

"A little."

"Beef?"

"What you looking for, John, dog meat?"

It was quiet.

"You got any of that?"

"Well, if you got your heart set on it, I can tell you where I buried my dog no more than a week ago."

Mr. John Barrow let out a sigh. "Won't be necessary," he said. "Jist curious."

◉ 3 ◉

Mr. Ben Riedlinger

Mr. Ben Riedlinger was kneeling in his garden, tying string to bean poles. He is a freckle-faced man with a kind of crooked nose, pretty much like Charley. And he is ready in a minute to fight or stomp when something doesn't go his way, just like Charley. Both of them spit when they get real mad.

Mr. Ben Riedlinger's practically my dad's best friend, and the two of them had some pretty good adventures when they were boys. Dad says one time they tried to see who could eat the most wild-onion sandwiches before getting sick. They would take a bite of the sandwich and cry a little bit. Then they would wash the taste out of their mouths quick with lemon soda pop and laugh their heads off. It was tie-all with the sandwiches when they both claimed they heard their mothers calling. Dad says he never told Mr. Ben Riedlinger, but he got sick before he even got home.

Mr. Ben Riedlinger looked up from tying the

poles. He's got a bad leg and he stood up to stretch it.

"Hello," I said.

"Can't talk, Pinch. Got to tie some of these beans before dark. Food is money, Pinch. A man's got to find any way he can to keep his family in good health." He looked up at me for a minute. "Sorry to be impolite, son, but the sun's slipping away."

"Were you really catching muskrats on my dad's land?"

"What's that, Pinch?" He thought about it for a minute. "Oh, well, son, your paw's been squawking about it, but it's between me and him and I don't care to discuss it with you. So move along. Charley's inside waiting for you."

Charley was helping his mom with the supper dishes. He isn't too happy working inside the house. I can't think of a time when he was happy working outside the house either.

"What *you* want?" he snapped when he saw me.

"Don't want a thing. You going to help me and Mr. John Barrow skin muskrats tomorrow?"

"Maybe." He wiped a plate with a dishrag. Then he looked up at me. "If you was to take another dishrag and help, I would finish faster and maybe I would tell you an important thing I have to tell somebody."

But Mrs. Riedlinger didn't like that idea at all.

"The people who soil the dishes are the people who clean them, Charley. I'm pretty sure I read that in the Bible somewhere. And if it ain't there, it should be." She turned to me and nudged me toward the door. "Charley will be finished in a minute, Pinch. At least he will be if he puts his mind to his job."

When Charley finally came outside, first thing he did was pick up a handful of dirt and rub his hands good to get the soapy smell off.

"Pinch, we got a problem."

"What kind of problem?"

"Chicken stealing and maybe worse," he said. "Somebody stole one of my paw's chickens two nights ago. And last night they came back and stole his brand-new saw right off the front porch. He's so angry, I've been keeping out of his way. And something else, Pinch. You just come with me." While we walked I told him about somebody stealing our chickens and Mr. John Barrow's too. It didn't bother him as much as his own being stolen. He led me to a place near his back fence where water from the pump drained and the ground was soft.

"Look at that!"

He pointed to a dent in the ground. It was like a man had been standing there on one foot, except that the footprint was too small for a man. It was more like a boy's.

◉ 4 ◉
Watching

"Pinch," Charlie said as we walked back toward his house, "I got a plan. You sleep at my house tonight and you and me can take turns watching to see if anything comes back after more chickens."

We went around to the front of the house to ask his mom, and there was Mr. Ben Riedlinger, sitting up straight in a chair on his front porch. He had a shotgun in his lap.

"Dad, what you doing?"

"I'm settling in for the night."

"On the front porch?"

"Any chicken stealing done tonight, I'm going to see they get their full share of my gratitude." He patted his shotgun.

"But me and Pinch planned to do the watching."

"No work for boys. You get to bed early and don't make too much noise doing it. I don't want you scaring the chicken stealer away."

Grown-ups don't want kids to have any fun. It's

been that way as long as I remember. But Charley's wasn't the only place with chicken-stealing problems. We ran all the way to my house to see if Mom would let Charley sleep over. When we got there, my dad was sitting on the front porch with a shotgun in his lap.

"Howdy, boys."

"You going to stay up watching?"

He nodded. "Seems like a good idea." He turned to Charley. "How's your paw doing with his trapping, Charley?"

"O.K." We started walking away.

"Pinch, before you go off anywhere, pen up your goat for the night. People who steal chickens might get bigger ideas. Put her in the drying shed. And put some straw in there too. Getting close to the time she'll be giving birth."

Work!

All the fun was draining out of the night. Maybe Charley could still sleep over, but pillow fighting wouldn't be half the fun of trying to waylay a chicken stealer. My goat Loretta wasn't too keen on being locked up in the shed, but we pushed her inside anyway. Then we went in the house for a glass of chocolate milk. But there wasn't any chocolate left.

"Pinch, Mr. John Barrow is surely going to need help watching his chickens."

It was Charley's idea, but I ran faster.

"Why," said Mr. John Barrow, "I'd be pleased as

a puppy dog with a saucer of warm milk if somebody strong and brave like you two boys would stay the night and help me keep watch."

We hurried back to tell our moms.

"You hungry, Pinch?" Mom asked me.

"Nope."

When we got to Charley's house, his mom gave him a slice of fresh peach pie. He said he wasn't ready to eat it yet, but if he was, it was too small a piece to share. Looked big enough to me.

By the time we got back to Mr. John Barrow's house, I was getting a little bit hungry. And him too. First thing we did was sit and watch Charley bite syrupy chunks out of his pie.

"Pie looks delicious, Charley," Mr. John Barrow said.

"Mmmmm," said Charley. He chewed slowly, not looking us in the eye.

When Charley was licking the last of the pie off his fingers, Mr. John Barrow jumped up and headed for the kitchen to dig in his pantry.

"Pinch, you and me got to find something to eat. Then we got to start thinking like chicken stealers. That way, we'll be one step ahead if anybody comes creeping around my yard tonight."

He found one apple and a half a loaf of stale bread in the pantry, and what he claimed was a hard-boiled egg on the mantelshelf. I wouldn't have broken that dusty egg open if I'd been starving for a week.

"Mr. John Barrow, if you are wrong about that egg being boiled, the smell will be so bad we won't be able to sleep in this house."

"Pinch, I boiled this egg myself. Why, it wasn't more than a week ago. I brought in two eggs from the hen house. I boiled one and I put the other one in my icebox for boiling later. I fried that one the very next morning. Then the day after that, I ate the boiled one. Why, son, I can even remember sprinkling a little salt on it. You jist got to use your head, Pinch. One egg fried, one made more tasty with a little salt. How many is that?"

"Two."

"I told you."

"Plus that mantelshelf egg equals three."

He looked at the egg in his hand.

"No, son, this is either got to be the fried egg or the egg with salt on it. I only had two eggs."

"Mr. John Barrow, that's a rotten egg you got in your hand. Unless some hen roosted on the mantelshelf while we were gone, that egg has probably been there maybe a year. You start to crack it, I'm getting out of here."

"Two of us," Charley yelled.

"Well, then, I don't have to decide right this minute. We can dine on the apple and bread. I'll just put the egg back where I found it and think some more about it if I get hungry again."

He cut the apple into halves. I took one. I wasn't

much interested in the stale bread. Charley eyed the other piece of apple but he didn't say a word.

When we had finished off the apple I was still kind of hungry. Mr. John Barrow made a pot of black coffee for himself and started dunking pieces of bread in the coffee. Looked mighty good. I do the same sometimes with coffee milk. But black coffee can rot your insides. That's what Mom says.

"We will take three-hour turns on the watch," Mr. John Barrow said. "That ought to git us right to sunup. Now, I'm wide-awake, and this coffee is going to keep me that way for a while, so I will go first. Who wants second watch?"

Charley said he didn't care and I said I didn't care and Mr. John Barrow asked us who didn't care the most. It looked about even to me, but he said Charley was the winner of second watch and I would have to settle for last. That was all right with me.

Mr. John Barrow decided to do his watching through the kitchen window, where he had a good view of the chicken yard when the moon was right. He locked the front and the back doors tight.

"I got to tell you boys. This back door don't lock too good. If you know the trick, you can git it open easy. All you got to do is take hold of the knob and lift and it pops right open."

He gave me and Charley a piece of blanket to help with the hardness of the floor. Then he turned off the light.

There were noises in the dark, but it wasn't really scary. Just frogs and maybe crickets and things like that. They sang me a lullaby and the next thing I remember is Charley shaking my shoulder.

"Wake up, Pinch. My eyes won't stay open another minute." He flopped out on the blanket and didn't make another sound.

All the lights in the house were out. Mr. John Barrow was probably snoring good in his bedroom. I felt my way into the kitchen and found the chair by the window. There wasn't any moonlight and I couldn't see a thing. Chicken stealers could've sneaked up on us and bashed us on the head before I even heard them coming. Not a sound. All I could hear was the early morning breeze moving the bushes outside the window.

The door creaked. I whipped around. Silence. I stood and eased over toward the door. It was probably the foolishest thing I did in my whole life.

I felt the edge of the door. Somehow it had popped open. I closed it softly and snapped on the lock. Charley had talked about how good he was at facing danger. Wait till he hears how I sat in the kitchen with the door unlocked, ready for whatever came my way. My knees were shaking a little bit, but I wasn't planning on telling him that. I sat back down in the kitchen chair.

There was a small noise at the door. The knob turned slowly. There was a half human sound, like something coming up from under fresh-dug dirt.

"Ughhh."

I streaked out of the chair and into the dining room.

"You keep out of here! You move and I'll shoot!"

"Don't do it," the half-human voice said.

"Charley! Mr. John Barrow!" I yelled. "Something's getting in!"

I wanted to run out the front door, but something might be waiting there too. I didn't even know where Mr. Barrow kept his shotgun.

"Wake up!" I yelled.

There wasn't even a piece of firewood to use as a club. I felt my way to the fireplace, looking for a poker. My hand touched the rotten egg on the mantelpiece.

There was a snap at the door. The lock sprang loose like Mr. John Barrow warned it might. I heard hinges squeak as the door slowly opened.

"I'll shoot!" I yelled.

"Quiet!" the thing snarled.

The door opened wide. A thing blacker than the dark outside stood in the doorway. A long, skinny thing. I let fly with the egg, using all the strength I had.

Smack! A hit! A smell filled the room that could've only come from the grave. Then a voice.

"Oh, Pinch, you shouldn't of done that!"

I jumped to put on the light.

Mr. John Barrow stood there, dripping rotten egg

all over his kitchen floor. Smell was worse than pole-cat frying in deep fat.

"I told Charley I was going out to check on the chickens!"

"He surely didn't say a word." I covered my nose from the smell.

"Well, he should've. Now I got to take another bath. That's two this winter already. Too much soap can poison a man."

Mr. Short

Nobody heard a single sound the rest of the night. But the stink of the place didn't help my sleep any. When I got home my folks were already eating breakfast.

"Pinch, there's a rotten-egg smell about you. Go wash up."

After breakfast, Charley and Mr. John Barrow came by. We walked our trapline and then we sat in my side yard under the oak tree and skinned musk-rats. It's a messy job. I had sliced into my own fingers so many times I didn't know if it was muskrat blood or Pinch Grimball blood I was looking at.

Suddenly there was a holler from the road. A little fat man got down off a wagon pulled by a frisky, chestnut horse. He tied the horse to a fence post that was almost as tall as him, then walked toward us, dragging a burlap sack. He sidestepped a muddy spot with his shiny knee-high boots. When he got close, he tipped his brown sporting cap and nodded.

"Good day to you," he said. His voice was strong and hard. There was a thin smile on his lips.

"My name is Short." He stared hard at us like he was daring us to snicker. "I'm passing through. Thought I would stop and say hello." Didn't look like he cared about it one way or the other. He let go of the sack, put his small hands on his hips, and looked around. His black eyes landed on the drying shed.

"Mind if I take a look?" Without waiting for an answer he walked over and stuck his little head in the door. It stayed inside long enough for him to have counted every single muskrat hanging in there. Then he turned around and walked back, shaking his head side to side.

"Trapping is a hard way to make a dollar," he said. "Never tried it myself, but I know it is so. Good thing there is money in it."

We had worked almost a month to get all those skins in the drying shed. Me and Charley started out thinking we would make some spending money. But when Mom said she was going to patch my old winter coat 'cause there wasn't a chance of buying a new one, I thought maybe I better help out. Charley and I could trap muskrats, sell the skins, and give the money to our folks. It felt good thinking about it.

When Mr. John Barrow asked if he could join up with us, it was plain what was on his mind. He would be the boss and we would do all the work. He is a pretty good trapper so we stood to learn from him, but he is also a crafty man, and if we didn't watch him close he would end up with his share and ours too.

Mr. Short bent over and picked up the neck of the sack he had been dragging.

"Guess you're wondering what I got in this sack?" He looked at each of us in turn, waiting for somebody to say something. I hadn't thought much about his sack, but when his eyes stared at me I nodded and he smiled his thin smile.

"If I could tell you, I would, but I can't. It's valuable, I'll tell you that." He started looking around again. His eyes lit on a cricket setting on the ground, not doing anybody a bit of harm. He walked over and stomped on it. He ground his foot in the dirt to make sure it was smashed up good. Then he came back to where he had been standing.

"Gentlemen," he said to all three of us, "in a minute I have to depart. I have an important meeting to attend. I may make a lot of money at that meeting. But I dare not bring this sack with me. I must find a safe place to leave it." He stared at us. It was like he was deciding if he could trust us. He sucked in air and pulled back his shoulders.

"Oh, a man's got to trust somebody," he finally said and tried to pull himself up a little taller. But all that fat around his middle wouldn't stretch, and he stayed mostly chubby.

"I will give each of you one silver dollar — " Suddenly he'd stopped talking. He bowed his head.

"I'm sorry, but I must leave." He turned and walked toward where his nervous horse was trying to chew the reins off the fence post.

Mr. John Barrow hopped up and ran long-legged after him, his hands red with muskrat blood.

"You got something you want done for money, you come to the right place. We three is the best there is at whatever you want."

Mr. Short took hold of the bridle. He stood there, clean and neat as a pin, looking up at tall, skinny Mr. John Barrow who was maybe a foot taller than him, needing a shave, hands all bloody and covered with grime.

"All right, sir, I will trust you." He turned about and the two of them walked back to where Charley and I were sitting. It was only then I noticed that Mr. Short hadn't even bothered dragging the burlap sack after him when he walked to the wagon.

"Guard this sack until I return and I will pay you well. I would prefer you didn't look inside." He stared Mr. John Barrow right in the eye. "You impress me as decent, trustworthy men. I will be back soon, perhaps a wealthy man."

He walked back to the road, unhitched his horse, and struggled to climb up into his wagon.

"Mr. Short!" Charley yelled at him and pointed at the wagon.

He turned his head and stared at us.

"Where'd you get the saw?" I looked where Charley was pointing. A brand-new saw was strapped to the side of the wagon.

"Bought it," he said, turning the wagon around the way he had come.

We watched until the wagon was out of sight. Then Mr. John Barrow dashed toward the sack.

"Don't touch it!" I yelled at him. He stopped.

"What, Pinch?"

"Two things. First, he said not to open it. Second, you don't wash your hands, you're going to get blood all over the sack."

"Well, excuse me," he said and ran gangly-legged toward the water pump.

"Mr. John Barrow!"

"Back in a minute, Pinch."

"We practically gave our word!"

"Why would we do that, Pinch?"

"Well, what about all this work we got to do?"

"Won't be a minute, Pinch." He came running back, grinning and wiping his hands on his shirt front as he ran. "I jist ain't good at surprises, boys. I want to see what he's got in that sack."

Truth is, so did I. The sack was tied at the neck with twine. He jerked it open and pulled it up to his face to look inside.

"Hmmmm!"

Then he stuck a long skinny arm inside and pulled something out. It was a piece of dark-brown fur. Mighty pretty fur. Not a bit like muskrat. He turned the sack upside down and dumped the contents on the ground. There were maybe a dozen silky dark-brown skins inside. I had never seen anything exactly like them before in my whole life.

A single white chicken feather lay in the midst of the furs.

Mr. John Barrow picked up one of the rich brown furs and rubbed it on his face.

"What's that chicken feather doing there?" I asked.

"How do you expect me to know that, Pinch? But I know something else. You know what these furs are? Mink, that's what. And mink is the most valuable fur there is. But I never saw mink as pretty as this around here."

"Dog!" said Charley.

"What, Charley?" Mr. John Barrow turned to him.

"Looks like dog fur to me. Maybe even Mr. Tony Carmouche's dog. He looked kind of like that."

Mr. John Barrow started at him. "People don't

stand guard over a sack of dog fur, Charley. Why would they do that?"

"Maybe they liked the dog," Charley told him.

"You wrong, Charley. That little man ain't one bit interested in dogs. This is fine mink. Maybe worth twenty dollars apiece." He stuffed the furs back in the sack. Then he put the sack down on the ground close to where he had been sitting so he could watch over it.

I went back to work, but I was thinking greedy thoughts, and a little bit ashamed. If Mr. Short came back we would get a dollar apiece. If he didn't, well, I guess the mink furs would be ours. My share might be nearly a hundred dollars. Dad could buy those goats he wanted and have money left over to keep food on the table at the Grimball house for the rest of the winter. I might even get a new winter coat and not have to go to school in patches.

Then there was the sound of a horse galloping. I jumped up and ran for the road.

⊙ 6 ⊙

Mrs. Long

"He's coming back!" I yelled.

But it wasn't him at all.

"Stop him! Stop him!" the rider screamed. But the horse wouldn't stop. I ran out in the road and waved my arms. It wasn't the smartest thing I've ever done. But that runaway horse took a look at me and slid to a stop, kicking up dust.

I stared at the sweating horse. It was a dead ringer for the frisky chestnut that had pulled Mr. Short's wagon. Then I lifted up my eyes and stared at the rider. She was the littlest woman I had ever seen. Maybe even the prettiest, too. She wore a flowery hat about a foot tall that must've been glued to her little head, 'cause not one flower was out of place.

Mr. John Barrow rushed around to help her off the horse. She stared hard at him, then gave him her hand and hopped down. But I got the feeling that this was a lady who didn't really need his help. She stood there, no taller than I was, dressed in riding britches and expensive-looking, soft leather boots. There was a ring on her finger with a green stone in it as big as a cat's eyeball.

She looked each one of us over, then fixed on Mr. John Barrow. She stared him straight in the eye longer than most people could stand looking at him, 'cause he is basically a skinny-nosed, ugly man.

"Thank you, sir," she told him.

She turned suddenly to me and smiled. "And you too, young man. What would I have done if you hadn't saved me?"

Then she looked closer at me and Charley, with our blood-red hands and smelling of muskrat. I stank worse before, but not much worse.

"My! What have you been doing? Who have you murdered?"

"Ma'am, we been skinning muskrats."

"Oh!" Pause. "Well, I suppose someone has to do it."

Mr. John Barrow tied her frisky horse to the fence post and the horse started chewing away at the reins.

"Now," the little lady said, "I suppose I should introduce myself. My name is Mrs. Long. Isn't that silly? But it's true. I'm on the way to visit my dear mother, who lives only a day's ride down the road." She had a mighty pretty smile. She looked around the yard, spotted a clean bench near where we had been skinning muskrats, walked over and sat down.

My goat Loretta had been resting up in a fork in the tree, watching what was going on. She hopped down, and stood next to the little lady. Mrs. Long stared at the gray goat. Her nostrils kind of twitched like she was testing the air for goat smell. If she'd known anything at all about goats, she'd know it's billy goats that smell bad, not nannies. She slid over on the bench away from Loretta and turned back to us.

"Now, you men just keep on doing what you were doing and I'll just sit here and rest a bit."

She looked straight at Charley.

"You have beautiful eyes."

A big grin popped on Charley's crooked-nosed face, and he dropped his *beautiful eyes* and started scratching lines in the dirt with his shoe.

She turned her head a mite and her eyes were staring straight into mine.

"And you. Oh, what can I say! If you hadn't saved my life!" It truly was the prettiest smile I ever saw. But the smile moved on.

"And you!" She clapped her hands together and stared into Mr. John Barrow's baggy eyes. "I could never have gotten off that vile horse by myself! Never!"

She looked all about her, suddenly flustered.

"I wonder if I might have a glass of water. I don't feel too well."

I jumped up to run and get it and fell over Charley trying to do the same. Mr. John Barrow beat us both to the water pump. He came back with a tin cup in his hand.

"My pleasure," he said, sickly smiling.

That tiny little lady raised the tin cup to her tiny little lips and took a tiny little sip. Then she offered the cup back to Mr. John Barrow.

"Thank you," she said in her soft, sweet voice. She began looking around again, taking in the muskrat skins, the pile of muskrat meat that we planned on boiling and maybe giving to the hogs, and the shed almost filled with drying pelts. Her eyes fixed on Loretta, daring her to come closer. Then her eyes shifted to the burlap sack.

"What's that?"

"It's a sack," Mr. John Barrow told her.

"Oh!" Her eyes moved to the pile of muskrat carcasses. She wrinkled her nose and turned away. "What a beautiful day," she said. Her head turned suddenly and her eyes fixed on Mr. John Barrow.

"What is your name?" she asked softly.

Mr. John Barrow straightened up. He took off his hat and smoothed back his hair. His smile was so big I thought it would pop his jaws. One thing he liked was getting attention from the ladies.

"Hee, hee," he said.

"That ain't his name," Charley said.

She waited patiently.

"Hee, hee," said Mr. John Barrow again. He shrugged his skinny shoulders like he was saying she really didn't want to know his name. Or else he forgot what it was.

"His name is Mr. John Barrow," Charley said.

Mr. John Barrow turned suddenly on Charley. His big smile shifted to a mean snarl. He put his skinny hands on his hips and stood over Charley like he wanted to squash him flat.

"*I* could have told her, Charley!"

"A kind name," Mrs. Long said. Mr. John Barrow turned back to her, his snarl curling into another big smile. "Many famous men have had that name." She fastened her eyes on him and wouldn't let go. She heaved her bosom and let out a sigh.

"A strong name," she said. "Are you strong enough to lift that sack?"

Mr. John Barrow nodded, but he wasn't interested in talking about the sack. He was waiting for her to say something else nice about him. She didn't say a word.

"My paw gave me that name," he told her.

"Marvelous," she said. Her eyes went back to the sack.

"Mr. John Barrow?" Her voice was soft as warm milk.

"Ma'am?"

"What is *in* that sack?"

"We are just holding it for a man. He said not to look inside."

"Oh!" She looked toward the front gate and checked up on her horse. It was still there, chomping on the reins. I never saw a horse so anxious to be someplace else.

"I love these flat, green lands," she said. "The

southland is truly a marvelous place. My own home is rocky and barren."

But she wasn't looking at the scenery. Something was on her mind and it wasn't flat pasture land with skinny cows on it. Her eyes were fixed on the sack. She wanted to know what was in it, but she was coming at the subject kind of sideways.

Mr. John Barrow listened to all the nice things she was saying about green grass, still hoping she would get back to talking about him.

"Four Corners is a pretty nice place," he said. "Been here all my life. Gits kind of hot sometimes, but I don't mind too much."

"The weather is just beautiful right now," Mrs. Long said. "Good for the mind. A thoughtful time, don't you think?"

Mr. John Barrow furrowed his brow and nodded his head like he was thinking hard, but my goat Loretta spends more time thinking than he does.

"And makes a person curious, too, don't you think?"

He nodded some more.

"Little things. Like what *is* in that sack?" She lowered her voice. "You do know, don't you?" She smiled her little smile. "Tell me?"

"Dog fur," Charley said sharply.

"What?" Her hands went to her face. "What would you want with a sack of dog fur?"

Mr. John Barrow slammed his hat on his head and

gave Charley a hard look. Then he turned to Mrs. Long.

"It ain't dog fur," he said. "Truth is, all we heard for sure is that it's worth plenty money and we been paid to watch over it. And not to look. He said not to look." He was looking down at the sack.

"Mr. John Barrow, look at me." Her words were slow and careful. He looked at her. "Now," her voice softened and she smiled at him. "Did you peek or not?"

He shrugged his shoulders and gave a little grin.

"It wasn't exactly a peek," he said.

"Then, tell me, Mr. John Barrow."

The little lady had turned him into taffy candy. He hopped up, untied the sack, and upended it.

◦ 7 ◦

Temptation

Mrs. Long threw herself to her knees in the rich brown furs. She grabbed a pelt in each hand and touched them to her face.

"Oh!" she cried. "I have never seen anything more beautiful." She knelt there for the longest while, her head down, the soft furs against her cheeks. When she lifted her head, there was a softness to her face, like she had been crying. But her eyes were like tiny balls of ice.

"I must tell you something," she said. "I am no innocent child when it comes to furs. My father was a trapper as you are. So I speak with some authority. What you are looking at is Catahoula fur. Taken from the depth of the swampland and most rare! These pelts are worth perhaps fifty dollars each." She stopped talking and clutched them to her breast.

"I must have them! Name your price. How many pelts are there?" Her bright eyes dashed about as she made a quick count. "I will give you five hundred dollars. No! You have been so kind. I will give you six hundred dollars!"

One third for me!

But it wasn't any good thinking on it. Those pelts belonged to Mr. Short. And he was coming back any time now.

Mr. John Barrow stuffed the pelts back in the sack, tied it tight, and handed it to her.

"Mr. John Barrow, what you doing? Can't sell what's not yours!"

"Pinch Grimball, you keep quiet. This little lady is got to have what's in this sack if she's going to be a happy little lady."

But he didn't push as hard as he sometimes does.

Mr. John Barrow isn't really a dishonest man. He's more a corners-cutting man.

Mrs. Long's pretty brown eyes moved from me to Charley to Mr. John Barrow. Maybe hoping. I watched back, wondering what her next move was going to be. When the talking stopped, she stood up and smoothed the skin under her eyes, like she was wiping tears away.

"All right, then. You certainly can't sell me what doesn't belong to you. You are honest men. But I would truly love to have these furs for my very own. I will return later today. And then we shall see what we shall see."

She walked toward the fence where her horse was still chewing on the reins. Mr. John Barrow ran after her to help her mount. Loretta trotted after him. Mrs. Long looked down at the goat.

"Why is your goat so bloated? Is it sick?" Loretta moved in close but Mrs. Long edged away.

"She is going to be a mother any day now," I told her, and patted Loretta on the head.

"Oh! Well, goodbye then. You are gentlemen, every one of you. I will return very soon." Mr. John Barrow took off his hat and gave her a big smile. She turned her horse around and moved slowly down the road.

Two things were crowding every other thought out of my mind:

The two littlest people in the world showing up in Four Corners on the very same day.

Mrs. Long going out of her way to make Mr. John Barrow think he was the salt of the earth.

I wasn't sure what was happening. But somebody knew something we didn't know. And we had better hold tight on to the sack of furs until we found out what it was.

◎ 8 ◎

Catahoula Fur

Mr. Short showed up midafternoon. His head was hanging about down to his knees. He climbed down from the wagon. It was a long climb for a short-legged man. I looked close at the horse that was pulling his wagon. For sure it was the twin of the one that had almost killed Mrs. Long.

This time he had a big dog with him, a round-headed, black-and-white spotted dog with glassy eyes. The dog started to follow him into the yard.

"Stay here, cur," Mr. Short told him and cuffed him on the side of the head. The big dog whined and sat. Then it saw my goat Loretta and showed teeth. That dog sat still in the road the whole time

Mr. Short was there, teeth bared, watching Loretta's every move.

"The Lord praise honest men," Mr. Short said when he spotted the burlap sack lying on the ground. Mr. John Barrow cracked a big grin as he watched Mr. Short walk over quickly and pick it up. "If only my fate and fortune were in the hands of good people like you." He drew open the sack and took a look inside.

"Gentlemen," he said, sliding his little hands in his pants pocket and turning his attention to us, "I am ruined. I don't even have the three dollars I promised you." He turned his pockets inside out so we could see he was telling the truth.

"I have only my honor and this burlap sack, filled with the promise of better things."

It stayed quiet for about a year. Mr. Short had run out of words, and we didn't know what to say. Another greedy thought was nudging me, but I didn't know if I wanted to entertain it. Then he started talking again.

"I have been cheated by evil men. All my money is gone. I don't even have the hundred dollars I need to return home to my lovely wife and children." His eyes pleaded with each of us in turn. Then his head nodded to his breast and he lifted his small hands to cover his face. He looked mighty sad.

The thought in my head began nudging all the harder. But Mr. John Barrow was the one to say it. Once it was out, it didn't sound right.

"We will be the ones to help," Mr. John Barrow told him. "We will buy that sack of dog fur you got there for twenty-five dollars, and you will be part-way back to where you want to git."

"Bless you, sir, but I couldn't do that. The furs in that sack are genuine Catahoula."

"We vote dog," Charley said.

"Catahoula! And not even ordinary Catahoula! Swampland Catahoula! I couldn't take less than a hundred dollars."

"You know the swamp is full of ticks?" Mr. John Barrow asked him, cocking his head sideways like he does when he is doing serious bargaining.

"What's that?" Mr. Short asked.

"Animals that live in the swamp git full of ticks. The little ticks git in there and dig the fur out, looking for a place to keep warm. Fur gits all mangy-looking after while."

"Sir, you've handled these beautiful furs. Did you see a single tick?"

"Little varmints are too small to see. Probably hiding. But maybe we can soak 'em in kerosene or something. I'll give you thirty dollars if you'll throw in some kerosene."

"I don't have any kerosene," Mr. Short said. "You can buy your own. But you soak these furs in kerosene, you'll ruin them. Maybe I could drop the price to ninety-five dollars, but that would be the very lowest."

Mr. John Barrow picked up the sack and opened it.

He pulled out one of the furs. Suddenly he dropped it, jumped back, and started scratching his hands together.

"I feel 'em! They crawling all over me!" He kept scratching and jumping around. But he kept one eye fixed on Mr. Short.

"All right," Mr. Short said, "enough of this. You cut out your dancing and I'll lower the price to seventy-five."

"Forty!" said Mr. John Barrow, jumping and scratching.

"Fifty!" said Mr. Short.

"Well . . ." said Mr. John Barrow, slowing down a little bit. Then he stopped altogether, walked over and picked up the fur again.

"All right," he said. "Now we only got one problem."

"Why, what is that?"

"I ain't seen that many dollars since I been a growed man. But you stuck your neck in the drying shed. And you can see we got more muskrat hides to trade than you can count. That is, if you are a trading man and not jist a prissy gentleman who has got to count his greenbacks."

Mr. Short kept his face perfectly straight, but for a second a tiny smile twitched in the corners of his mouth. Maybe he was happy. I sure wasn't. I had been trapping and skinning and racking muskrats forever. Charley and I had done good. If we kept working hard, we might even be rich some day. But becoming one-third owner of a sack of dog fur wasn't a move in the right direction. Besides, my dad was counting on buying those new goats. And I wouldn't mind a new winter coat and eating bread whenever I wanted.

Mr. John Barrow and Mr. Short counted every skin in the drying shed.

"You get out of that shed," I yelled at them. "One third is mine and one third is Charley's."

"Well, Pinch, Mr. Short here needs help bad. We got these skins we ain't using. Ours are worth more than what's in the sack, but it's the spirit of the thing. Pinch, Charley, you see what I'm saying, don't you?" But we both just stared at him.

"Boys," Mr. Short said, "no need to worry about it. If you don't have cash money, there won't be any business. Do you think I am a dumb man? Do you think I will be taken advantage of?"

His eyes roamed to the tree where Loretta was perched. He walked over to a small pine in the side yard and pulled off a handful of needles. Then he came back and offered them to Loretta. She snorted, then hopped down out of the tree and ate the pine needles from his hand.

"What about throwing in this pregnant goat?" Mr. Short asked.

I shook my head hard enough to loosen my ears. Loretta was a milk goat and Dad said she was going to pay for herself before the winter was over. Anyway, she was my friend, and you don't trade away your friends.

"I tell you what, Pinch and Charley," Mr. John Barrow said. "I will trade my third of the muskrat hides for that mink fur. Then when you boys are spending your share on a sack of penny candy, I'll be buying a wagonload of chocolate fudge."

"What if the furs are dog?"

"Pinch," Mr. John Barrow said. He turned his back on Mr. Short and kept squinching his face and winking one eye at me. "Son, we got to help out this poor man. These furs of his ain't worth much. They might even be dog, like Charley says. But they are sure worth more than that cud-chewing goat of yours. And the most important thing, Pinch, is to help this little man git back to his little children." He started squinching and winking again. "Besides, Pinch, you seen these furs. If they was fixed up right, they might make some *little lady* happy."

But my head wasn't screwed on sideways and I told him so. I'll trade one dollar for five any day, if I get to take a good look at the five before the trading is done. But not if it's hiding in a burlap sack.

Right then Mom stuck her head out of the back door and called me in for lunch. Charley said he was a little bit hungry too, and so he would go home. But he'd be back pretty quick.

I walked toward the house. Mr. John Barrow and Mr. Short moved to the bench under the tree and sat down, still chatting away. I couldn't hear what they were saying, but I didn't trust Mr. John Barrow more than a half inch. I whipped around and went back to listen. When I got close, Mr. John Barrow stopped talking.

"What you want, Pinch?"

"Trading talk is over till me and Charley finish eating lunch."

"We jist talking about weather, Pinch."

The minute I turned my back, they started jawing again, but softly like they didn't care for anybody to hear what they were saying. I could only hear the buzz of their voices while Mom and I were eating. Afterward she put me to washing canning jars, and I couldn't hear a thing.

Then a screech louder than a bobcat split the day in two.

⊙ 9 ⊙

Mean and Crafty

I rushed outside to see what was happening. Mr. Short was gone. So was his wagon. Mr. John Barrow sat on the bench under the tree, the burlap sack at his feet.

"We going to be rich, Pinch!" he shouted when he saw me. He sounded like a happy man. But Charley wasn't happy one bit. He stabbed his finger at me and yelled.

"You know what happened while you were in there getting fat on bread and jam? This ornery man traded muskrat for dog, that's what. We lost every one of our muskrat furs, that's what. And it's all your fault for not being here to watch over him, that's what!"

Mr. John Barrow stretched tall and held up the sack.

"You boys all wrong. You got to see things my way. That little lady offered us more money than I ever seen in my whole life. When she gits back it's all ours."

I glared at him. The door to the drying shed was open. Loretta stood in the doorway, looking out to see what all the yelling was about.

"You see what I'm saying, don't you, Pinch?"

Charley stomped the dirt. "You shouldn't of let him alone, Pinch. You ought to know he'd pull some kind of foolishness."

"Mr. John Barrow," I yelled at him, "you said you were talking about the weather."

"Why, we was, Pinch. Whether to trade or not to trade."

"I swear, Pinch, you a dumb one," Charley said.

"Charley, shut your mouth." I had better things to do than listen to him. I was twisting and grinding my mind to think like Mr. John Barrow. I had been tricked by him so many times I don't get mad anymore. I get crafty. He stood there, watching us. He probably liked watching a fight he wasn't a part of.

"Shouldn't call me ornery, Charley. Ornery ain't rich. We gonna be rich, you wait and see." He sat down on the bench.

Charley was red-faced. He stared at Mr. John Barrow. It was a good idea. I stared at him too. In a little while he started twitching in his seat. He scratched the side of his neck. He cocked his head. He looked at me and saw that I was staring. He turned his head and saw Charley was doing the same.

"She'll be here any minute now, boys."

He turned his head away from us, searching the ground for a twig or a rock or something else to fiddle with so he wouldn't have to look us in the eye.

"Did you trade Mr. Short that bale of special fur over in the corner of the shed?" I asked him, mean and crafty.

"Weren't no special furs in there, Pinch. Just muskrat."

"Mink. A whole bale. My dad's been holding on to them, waiting for the price to go up. He's going to sell them tomorrow."

He jumped up and ran to the drying shed, pushing Loretta aside as he stuck his head in the door.

"It ain't here, Pinch!"

"Over in the far corner," I told him.

He went inside and walked to the back of the shed.

I slammed the door shut and threw the bolt.

"Pinch, I can't see too good with the door closed. But it's gone. I can see that. Lord, Pinch, you're dad'll kill me!"

. I grinned at Charley and he grinned back and the two of us went and sat down under the tree to wait for Mrs. Long. The shed door rattled.

"Pinch, the door is stuck. I can't git out of here."

Silence.

"Charley?"

Silence.

"All right, now, you two boys trying to play a trick on me. That's right, ain't it. Well, I ain't in no hurry. Three can play that game."

I could hear him shuffling around in the shed. Then there was a plop as he sat down on the floor near the door.

Silence.

"Pinch? You tell your goat not to stare mean at me."

"Seems like she's got a right to stare where she wants to. One thing about that goat. She knows who her friends are."

"Well, I'm not going to sit in this smelly shed and git mean stares from a goat. Now, you let me out of here."

Silence.

"Pinch, maybe your goat's jist hungry. Why don't you let her out and go feed her a few tin cans with ragged edges?"

I stopped listening to him. I wanted it quiet. I wanted to be able to hear Mrs. Long's horse galloping toward us when it was still far down the road. She would be coming soon. I hoped it was so. The furs weren't dog. She would hand over the money and when me and Mom and Dad sat down to dinner, I would plunk all those dollars down in the center of the table. Then I would sit back and watch their eyes sparkle.

Nothing was coming down the road.

She promised she would come back. She said she *had* to have the furs.

Suppose it was a fib.

We sat until our bottoms went to sleep, but Mrs. Long never showed.

◉ 10 ◉

Mr. Tony Carmouche

It's hard work, trying to out-mean somebody. I was tired of sitting. And I was tired of being mean and crafty. I don't see how Mr. John Barrow gets so much pleasure out of it.

"Pinch, when you going to let me out?"

"When you going to say you're sorry?"

"Why, boys, I couldn't be any sorrier than I am right now if I was going to turn into a puppy dog at sunup. Now, nobody could be sorrier than that."

"And you got to be the one to tell my dad the furs are gone."

"I'll stay in here with the goat, Pinch."

"Then we'll wait till he gets home and I'll tell him you got something to say."

"Don't do it, Pinch. I'll tell him like you want me to, but you got to let me pick my time."

When I opened the shed door, Loretta came crashing out first. Mr. John Barrow had been doing all the complaining about being locked up with the goat, but the goat hadn't been too keen on the idea either.

We sat and waited some more. When Mr. Tony Carmouche came out and started sweeping off the front porch of his store, Mr. John Barrow decided to go over and have a chat. Me and Charley followed. He told Mr. Tony about Mr. Short trading him the furs and he dug in the sack and showed them to him.

Mr. Tony took a good look at the furs. He felt one of them on both sides. He touched it to his face. He sniffed at it. Mr. Tony isn't only the storekeeper. He is also the deputy sheriff and the postman. He's got more book learning than anybody else in Four

Corners, except maybe the schoolteacher, and you could see the brain wires humming.

"Smells like dog," he said. He gave the skin back to Mr. John Barrow.

We just stood there, long-faced, staring at him. It wasn't what we wanted to hear.

"Can't imagine why you three would trade good muskrat for dog."

Then Mr. John Barrow told him about Mrs. Long.

"Looks like you got skinned," Mr. Tony said, going back to his sweeping.

"What you mean?"

"John, there's always someone sitting and waiting to find a greedy man. You know why? 'Cause greedy men take risks they don't need to, that's why. They put dollars before sense, that's why." He thought about what he had said for a moment. "You know, that's pretty good. Have to remember that one." Then he turned back to us.

"John, you need any feed for that blind mule of yours?"

"Mule's gone. Just walked off. I don't plan on buying any more feed till I find him. Still thinking of shooting him anyway."

Mr. Tony whacked the broom on the porch rail to get the dust out of it.

"You heard about what happened to that Jenkson Jones fellow who works at the sawmill? Practically the same as you three. Traded about a hundred furs for a map to some buried treasure. He dug till he was over his head and all he found was water and crawfish.

"I'm telling you, these are bad times. People are roaming about trying to get hold of your money and my money and anybody's money any way they can. Honest or otherwise. People are skinning the muskrat skinners."

He went back to sweeping for a while.

"Pinch, that goat of yours has been wandering out in the road all by herself. You better pen her up. Fat goat like that would be mighty tempting to a hungry stranger."

More sweeping.

"If I was you boys, you know what I'd do?"

"What?"

"I'd sew those skins together and make a blanket. At least it would keep you warm until all the dog hair fell out."

◉ 11 ◉

Scapegoat

Next morning, Charley and I headed for Mr. John Barrow's. He had said he wanted to sleep on it before he told Dad about the furs being gone. Well, he had slept on it.

He was sitting on his front steps, cracking pecans with an ax. He waved and grinned when he saw us.

"You want to crack pecans with me, Pinch and Charley?"

"No," we told him. I was almost hoping he'd smack his finger.

"Well, don't expect to eat any then." He gave a pecan a little tap and nothing happened. He hit it another little tap. The pecan rolled around a little bit. He hauled back and gave it a good hit with the ax and smashed it flat, meat, shell and all.

"Little varmint," he said, and reached for another. But before he gave it a hit, he looked up at us and grinned.

"I seen that little fellow again," he said softly. "He was sneaking around down by Judge Ridley Boudreaux's house when I spotted him. Had that ornery dog with him too. Nearly took a piece out of my leg."

I never expected to see that little man again. If we could get hold of him, maybe we could get our furs back.

"You think he's still there?"

"He's long gone, Pinch. Said he had business down the road. We had a nice chat. Pretty good fellow. Look what he gave me." He put the ax down, stuck his hand in a paper sack that was sitting on the top step, and pulled out a single muskrat hide.

"Said he was sorry we were disappointed with our

trade, and he'd be happy to trade back again any time we wanted. Only thing is, somebody stole all them furs from him. Ain't that awful? That little man was almost crying, he was so sad." Mr. John Barrow put the lonely hide back in the sack and stood there, scratching his head.

"Who stole them from him?" I asked. "Was it strangers? Which way did they go?"

"I don't know answers to all them questions, Pinch. You think I got nothing to do but ask that man questions?

"But you listen to this. Him and me got to talking about how hard times were in Four Corners. He said if we wanted, he would help make things better."

"Mr. John Barrow, I wouldn't trust that man as far as I could throw a bucket of spit."

He shuffled closer to me and put his hand on my shoulder.

"Pinch, what he said made some sense. You want to hear or don't you?"

"Not me," I told him.

"Me neither," Charley said.

"Well, I'm gonna tell you anyway." He leaned closer and went back to talking like he was telling secrets.

"He said that your goat Loretta would solve all the problems."

"What?" Now he had me listening. He knew it and grinned ear to ear.

"He said he read about it someplace. A long time

ago whenever a town like Four Corners was in trouble, the people would git theirselves a goat. They would load all their troubles on the back of the goat. Then they would git rid of the goat."

I waited for him to finish the story.

"That's it, Pinch. That's how to do it. Now, don't that make some sense? And that little man said if we would jist give him the goat, he would take care of all the rest of it."

His head works like a windup toy, is what it is. When he is after something he wants, like a dollar, his head winds up fast and furious. Rest of the time, his head is kind of unwound.

"Mr. John Barrow, if we give Loretta to Mr. Short and he takes care of all our troubles, do we get Loretta back?"

"He said he would take the goat out into the wilderness, Pinch."

"Which way is the wilderness?" Charley asked him.

"Charley, he didn't tell me everything." He started scratching his belly like he does sometimes.

"Mr. John Barrow, did he tell you what *you* would get if you gave him the goat?"

"What's that, Pinch?"

"You heard me!"

"Why, Pinch, you think I would try to make a profit with all the suffering going on?"

I nodded my head up and down, but he wasn't even looking at me. He was shuffling his feet around.

Then he bent over and picked up a stick and started fooling with it.

"You going to tell us what your profit would be?"

"Son, I really like that goat of yours. It's a friendly sort of goat. I wouldn't do one thing to harm it. But times is hard. Mr. Short said he would give me a dollar or a one-third share in his chestnut horse, whichever I wanted. Except, I could have a piece of legal paper saying the horse was one-third mine then and there. But if I wanted the dollar, I'd have to wait till next week."

I was tired of foolish talk. I told him that Loretta wasn't the kind of goat that wanted to give up tree climbing, even if it meant that everybody in Four Corners would eat regular again.

"Where you plan on meeting him?" I asked.

"He said he had to keep moving, but he'd be in touch."

"Well, me and Charley are going to find him. That's for sure. But first you come on home with me and tell my dad about the furs."

"Pinch, I didn't sleep too good last night."

"You come on anyway."

"Wouldn't do a bit of good for me to go to your house, Pinch. I wouldn't know what to do when I got there. That's the problem about missing my sleep. Maybe if I sleep good tonight, I could go to your house tomorrow."

I didn't want to wait until tomorrow. Mainly

'cause there were going to be more tomorrows after that.

"If I tell my dad, he is going to come after you with a stick. If you tell him, he'll stomp and yell and maybe that's all."

He didn't move an inch.

"You'd better come on. He's putting a new handle on a sledgehammer right this minute. It would make a good stick if he needed one."

He shook his head like he wasn't going to do it. But then he took one cautious step in the right direction.

"He's using solid oak," I said to keep him moving.

"It wasn't really my fault, Pinch. That little man's got a tongue that could talk the stand-up ears off my mule."

We were moving, slow, but in the right direction.

"Did I tell you boys about my poor mule?" He slowed down, then stopped. "Maybe I ought to go back and start looking for him right now."

"I saw my dad hit a cypress fence post with a piece of oak one time. Broke the post in two."

He looked at me. Then he started walking again.

⊙ 12 ⊙

The Seeing-Eye Goat

Dad wasn't out in the yard working on the sledge-hammer handle and angry about something like I had hoped he would be. We went into the kitchen, and he was there, wearing one of Mom's aprons and peeling potatoes. Worse still, he was even smiling.

"Hello, John, how about some coffee?" Dad said.

"Dad, Mr. John Barrow hasn't got time to drink coffee. He wants to tell you something important." Dad went over and got a cup and filled it with hot black coffee anyway. Mr. John Barrow smiled and took a sip. Then he started talking, but he didn't say a thing about the furs.

"I been telling these boys about my blind mule," he said. "He's a pretty good mule, but he can't even see to walk from his shed to the pasture. I got no use for a blind mule. Can't work or nothing. He is going to stumble around and git hisself hurt bad. Maybe nothing left to do but shoot him, less I can git your help."

Dad put down his knife and smiled at Mr. John Barrow.

"I don't have no use for a blind mule, John."

"I don't want to sell him. What I was hoping is that I could borrow that ugly goat of yours. Maybe I could teach the goat to lead the mule to pasture. I really don't want to shoot him if I don't have to. Kind of like the critter."

"Never heard of a seeing-eye goat before, John. That don't mean it won't work. But Loretta is pregnant and I don't want nothing to happen to her. You better let me think on it. I'll let you know in a day or two."

"Well, what am I going to do with the mule until you make up your mind?" Mr. John Barrow set the coffee cup down on the table.

"I guess you'll have to take care of your own mule," Dad said. "Think of that."

"Dad, Mr. John Barrow wants to tell you something," I said.

"I'm listening," Dad said.

"I ain't got time to do any more talking right now," Mr. John Barrow said. "I got to go and find my mule and take care of him like your dad told me to, Pinch." He smiled all around and headed for the door.

"Mr. John Barrow!"

"We'll do it tomorrow, Pinch." He opened the door.

"Let him go, Pinch," Dad said. "Almost time to

eat lunch. Anyway, later on we got to haul the furs you got in the drying shed to where mine are in Judge Ridley Boudreaux's barn."

Mr. John Barrow turned and gave Dad a curious look. Then he walked out and quickly closed the door behind him.

When we sat down to eat, I started to tell Dad about the furs. But I couldn't do it. I looked at him. He was staring at two pieces of bread on the table in front of him. But he didn't touch them. Finally he lifted his head and looked at me and all of a sudden I remembered Mr. Short's idea of sacrificing my goat Loretta to help Four Corners. I told Dad about it.

"That man's up to something fishy," Dad said. "Sure, son, maybe they did that a long time ago. But people change. Now, you look a-here." He stopped talking for a second while he put a heaping spoon of sugar in his coffee. "Long time ago people believed in monsters and things like that."

"Still got monsters," I told him.

He looked at me over the rim of his coffee cup.

"What you mean?"

"Regular monsters. Whatever's been stealing everybody's chickens. No blood. No feathers. Nothing. Just like monsters."

"Aw, Pinch, it's just a hungry tramp. Or maybe even a hungry neighbor. Let me finish what I was saying." He took a sip of coffee, put the cup down, and settled back in his chair. I glanced down at my plate to see how much food was left. The chop was gone but I still had half a boiled egg and a piece of bread with one bite out. I had to make it last.

"Now, let's see," he said, rubbing the palms of his hands on his rough cheeks. "Tony put an idea in my head a while back and I been chewing on it ever since. Long time ago, Pinch, people didn't understand plenty things. So they made up monsters and dragons and maybe they even killed goats when things got bad. When they didn't understand what was going on, they would turn to make-believe. It's like they were children way back then and we are grown-ups now." He finished off his coffee. "When I was your age I played as much as you do. I worked as little as I had to, same as you. But a person changes, Pinch." He stood up. "You know, I think I got time for one more cup of coffee." He went over to the stove and poured himself a cup.

I swallowed the last of my egg and bread. Now I would just have to sit and grow roots.

"Pinch, I never did tell you about a dog I had when I was about your age. Name was Bump."

Mom laughed softly, and Dad looked over at her and smiled. He came back to the table and sat down.

"Told your mom. Well, me and that dog worked every wood and field for two miles around, stirring up rabbits and birds. We did it every single day for almost a year. But, son, Bump wasn't a real dog. Bump was in my head. Then Ben Riedlinger's family moved to Four Corners, and I didn't need an imaginary dog to play with anymore."

I never had an imaginary dog. Had a real dog one time. But pigs and goats are more to my liking.

"Son, the thing that's wrong in Four Corners is simple enough. There ain't enough money to keep bread on the table. Killing goats won't help. Only two kinds of suffering I can think of that will." He looked at Mom again. "Your mom already told you one kind. When we don't have, we just do without. I been trying my best to show you the other kind. It's called plain old hard work. You want something or you need something, you give a try at selling goat milk. You work your traps harder. You look for work chopping wood or mending fences or whatever it is you can do."

I heard what he said. I pretty much understood. You got to decide what you want, and you got to work hard at it. I can do it some of the time.

"Clean off your plate, son, and get on out in the yard. There's a post rotting in the back fence. See if you can get it out of the ground."

⊙ 13 ⊙

Cat Eyes

After I cleaned my plate I went outside to check on Loretta, but she wasn't anywhere to be found. Dad was in the backyard, working on his traps.

"You seen Loretta?" I asked him. He stood up and looked all around the yard.

"That goat's your worry, Pinch, not mine."

"I can't find her."

"Where you been, Pinch? Maybe she followed you."

"Haven't been anyplace."

"Lord, Pinch, a million things could happen to a goat. You just can't let a pregnant goat run loose. We better go look."

When we got around the corner of the house, Loretta was standing there waiting for us. There was a short rope around her neck. At the other end of the rope was the tallest, grayest man I had ever seen. He even had a grayish-white hat on his head. He stood there, looking at us with eyes that were slanty and partly closed, like a cat trying to get used to the bright light of day.

"This your goat?" he asked. His voice was heavy. "Found her way down the road." There was a pleasant smile on his face.

Dad stared at him. He walked over and took the rope.

"We was just starting to look." Dad removed the rope from around her neck and Loretta walked a few steps and began chewing away on the leaves of a small tree. She made a grunting sound. I looked at her. Dad did too.

"Something wrong here," he said slowly. He put his hand on her belly. But I could see from where I stood what was bothering him.

"The goat's delivered her kids!" he shouted. "Mister, what you know about that?"

The tall man with cat eyes shook his head side to side.

"She was a little wobbly when I first found her, but that was all. Weren't any little goats around. Maybe they're back in the swamp someplace."

Dad faced him, head high, hands on hips.

"Stranger," he said, "just who are you and where you come from?"

"Name's O'Toole," Cat Eyes said. "And I didn't come here just to bring back your goat. I want to ask for your help." He reached into his pocket, pulled out a piece of paper and handed it to Dad.

"My job is to protect the law," he said. "That's

what it says on the paper. I been chasing after two people a long time now. Both of them about this big." He held his hand up in the air about as high as my head. "You seen anybody like that?"

There was a puzzled look on Dad's face. He didn't say anything.

"You find out where they are or what they are doing, you send for me before you do anything. I'm renting a room from Judge Ridley Boudreaux for a couple of days."

Cat Eyes O'Toole took back his piece of paper, stuck it in his pocket, nodded goodbye, and walked back to the road.

◉ **14** ◉

Sharing

Dad sent me to lock Loretta in the drying shed. Somebody was going to have to tell him that the shed was empty. Mr. John Barrow always had hurry-up business to do whenever he saw my dad coming. It would have to be me.

Dad had me help him hang wet muskrat traps on

Mom's clothesline, where they would rust lightly and lose their shine.

"What you think of that skinny man, Pinch?" he asked.

Before I had a chance to answer, Charley and his dad walked up the steps of Mr. Tony's store, planning to do some shopping. When Dad saw Mr. Ben Riedlinger, he yelled out.

"Ben, you wait up!"

"Hi, Pinch," Charley yelled and I yelled "Hi" back to him.

The two of them waited on the porch of the store. Dad walked over and stopped about ten feet away.

"I asked you once. Now I'm telling you. Don't trap on my land."

Mr. Ben Riedlinger stood there, not saying a word, but getting red in the face and glaring back at my dad, glare for glare.

"Well?" Dad said. "I'm waiting for you to say something."

Mr. Ben Riedlinger limped down the porch steps and faced my dad. They were both big men, standing face to face, glaring but not saying a word. Both of them were showing plenty of teeth, fists clenched at their sides.

Finally Charley's dad broke the silence.

"Will, I didn't expect this from you."

"That's my trapping land," Dad said.

"We been friends a long time. We shared before."

"I ain't talking about what happened before. I got

a family to take care of. I can't remember a winter when it was harder to earn a dollar. I make my living from trapping and you don't."

Mr. Ben Riedlinger shook his head side to side very slowly, like he was saying it wasn't so.

"Will?"

"What?"

"Last winter when you cut your foot with the ax, it was me that shot the deer that kept meat on your table."

"And it was me that chopped enough wood to keep your stove lit the rest of the winter," Dad said.

"I never asked you to."

"That's right, you didn't. But you used the wood."

Mr. Ben Riedlinger stomped his foot.

"Will?" He stared hard at my dad.

"What?"

"I got a family to take care of, same as you."

He turned around and walked down the road. Dad pulled in a chest full of air like he planned on doing some loud yelling. He curled his hands into big fists. But he didn't say one word. He kind of snorted out the air. Then he walked back to where we had been working on the traps.

Charley and I stood there and looked at each other. I wasn't mad at him and he wasn't mad at me. His dad was already a good piece down the road. Charley turned to his dad. He turned back to me. Then he walked slowly after his dad.

It was time for me to go help Dad. I looked back

one time. Charley was still walking, but he was looking this way. When he saw me looking at him, he
turned his head again.

I wanted to yell, "So long!"

I wanted to yell, "See you later!"

I wanted to yell, "It's our dads that are mad. Not
us."

But I didn't say a thing.

◎ 15 ◎

Emptiness

Dad walked into the backyard. I started to follow
him but went into the kitchen instead. Mom looked
at me like she was trying to read my face. I didn't
know what to tell her. Everybody was fighting with
everybody. It wasn't like Four Corners at all.

"I don't feel so good, Mom. Could I have a glass
of milk?"

She poured the milk. Then she leaned over and
kissed me lightly on the cheek.

I sat at the table, looking out the window. I remembered things. There was a party we had when I

was maybe seven. It was the first party I ever remember having. But it rained and nobody came. I cried hard until Mom put the first spoonful of ice cream in my mouth. Then I didn't cry anymore. But I still remember.

My dog Spot got killed while trying to cross the road right in front of my very own house. He was more of a pup than a dog. Me and Dad dug a hole in the backyard and buried him. I held him close and laid him deep in the brown dirt myself. Spot wasn't warm anymore. Holes in the ground are scary when you start throwing dirt back in them. I never did get me another dog.

Now, bad things are happening again.

Mr. Ben Riedlinger and my dad are fighting. That shouldn't mean me and Charley have to fight too. Charley is my friend. You ought not have to fight with your friend if you don't want.

I sipped the milk. It was warm. It didn't taste good.

Dad was in the backyard. I could see him out the window. I had forgotten to take care of the rotten fence post and he was doing it. His big hands reached out and grabbed hold of the post. He shook it left and right. I put my milk glass down and went to help.

He dug his feet into the ground and smashed his shoulder into the post. It snapped clean at ground level. He dropped the wood and stood back a step. There was a big smile on his face.

"First good thing that's happened today," he said.

Then he stepped back one more step. His smile faded. "I didn't want to do that! Now it's going to be twice as hard to get the rotten part out."

We worked another hour before we got that piece of rotten wood out of there. We dropped another strong, new post in the hole, packed the dirt tight, and restrung the wire. Until the job was almost finished, he didn't say another word.

"This ain't a good day," he said, "and I got a feeling it's gonna get worse." He smacked the hammer and drove a staple into the wooden post. "I need more staples, Pinch. We got any in the drying shed?"

He walked toward the drying shed where all the muskrat hides were supposed to be. He put his hand on the door handle.

"You know, son, I want to be sure you understand what's happening between me and Ben. I'm right about that being my land. Why, you listen to this. I even paid for the right to trap on that land." He looked me in the eye. "You know where I was before supper last night? 'Course you don't. Me and some of the other men around here who *do* trap regular had a meeting with a railroad man. He told us there was a new law that said a fellow has to pay the railroad to trap on their land. He had all the fancy legal papers to prove it. That little man took ten dollars from every one of us, and he said that only gave us the right to trap for this season. Twenty years I been trapping around here and now I got to pay ten dollars for a piece of paper that says I got a right to do it.

"Worse still, I had to pay it to a fat little man who didn't even know the difference between a number one trap and a number four."

He shook his head slowly, turned around, and reached for the door handle.

I trembled. If he found out the hides were gone before I said anything, it would look like I'd been afraid to tell him. But I wasn't afraid.

"And now a lawman comes by and says to watch out for little people," he said.

We had worked hard for those hides. Dad had been happy with me when I told him we were trying to help. He was counting on me. I wanted him to believe that I could help.

"Dad," I called softly to him. It had to be now.

He turned and looked at me.

"There aren't any furs in the shed, Dad."

The tears came. I couldn't stop them as I told him about Mr. Short and the sack of dog fur. He stared at me. He listened to my every word, slowly shaking his head side to side. The only questions he asked were about Mr. Short.

"Tell me what he looked like. How did he talk? What did he say?"

Suddenly he thundered!

"Ho-lee-gee!" He picked up a steel trap, pulled back his arm and splattered the trap against a tree. He turned, pulled open the door of the drying shed, and stuck his head inside. I stood there and waited, wiping tears that wouldn't stop. I prayed for a miracle that would fill the shed to the rafters with the finest furs he had ever seen. But it wasn't to be. He closed the door and turned to me.

"Dumb thing you did, Pinch. And John Barrow's got some explaining to do. That extra money would've helped." But there wasn't any more loud talk. He reached over and put his arm around my shoulder. He pulled me close.

"We still got enough furs stored in the Judge's barn to make it through the cold weather, Pinch. I got a good lock on the door to the loft. The furs are safe." He looked sideways at me. "You ain't told anybody where they are, have you?"

I hadn't told a soul. But I was pretty sure Mr. John Barrow had heard Dad talking about where they were. I told him so.

"John wouldn't steal my furs, Pinch."

He wouldn't steal them, but he might tell.

"Son, it's really me I'm mad at. Looks like the same little man took me too. I'm ten dollars poorer to prove it. I got to do some thinking. This ain't the way Four Corners ought to be."

He gave me a little push and walked off. He rounded the side of the house. Then he turned and came back.

"You and John and Charley lost your furs trying to make a lot of money without working for it. All I did was try to obey the law. I don't want you to take any joy from the fact that both of us got took. If you want to learn from me, you watch where I put my feet. But if I put one of mine in a cow pie, you try to find another spot to put yours."

He looked at me, asking if I understood, and I nodded.

"Son, let's walk over to the Judge's barn."

We stopped on the road in front of the Judge's house. It's a big, white one set back off the road and surrounded by bushes and flowers and oak trees. He's the closest thing to being rich we got in Four Corners.

Next to the house is a pasture where he keeps his goats and a cow or two. On the other side of the pasture is his big red barn.

Dad pulled the barn doors wide. He opened the large, shiny lock on the door leading to the loft stairs and we went up. One end of the loft was stacked high with bales of muskrat fur. He pointed over to a corner where the stack was low.

"That's where I was going to put yours, Pinch. But what's done is done. Only reason I brought you here was to make sure you didn't spend a lot of time worrying. When I sell these, we'll make it fine. It's my job to see that we do." He folded his arms across his chest and just looked. Then he turned and moved toward the stairs.

"Now, let's get on home," he said and gave me a swat on the bottom.

◉ 16 ◉

Fortune Telling

I lay in bed that night, thinking instead of sleeping. What to do? When I woke up in the morning, I had a piece of a plan. Mr. John Barrow was the last one to see Mr. Short. I hadn't been dumb enough to give him Loretta. But suppose I had? What would Mr. John Barrow have done?

They had to have a meeting place picked out!

Muskrat furs, here I come!

I knocked hard on Mr. John Barrow's front door. There wasn't a sound coming from inside. I knocked even harder. The door opened slowly, but only partway.

"What you want, Pinch?" His eyes were narrow and suspicious.

"Something."

"Still don't feel too good, Pinch. Can't go visiting your paw." He bent himself over like an old man, showing how poorly he felt.

"I already told him."

His head jerked up, eyes looking this way and that.

"Is he coming after me with a stick?" He's always been a little afraid of my dad.

"I hope. Right now I want to talk to you about the little people."

Eyes popped open.

"What you want with them?"

A chair scraped inside the room and a voice called to Mr. John Barrow, but he didn't pay it any mind. Suddenly Mr. Short's head stuck out the partly opened door.

"You!" he said. "Inside! This very minute!"

Mr. John Barrow opened the door wide and I walked into the living room. The shades were down and it was dark, with only a single kerosene lamp to light the room.

Mrs. Long sat over in one corner behind a small table. Soft and hazy light flickered around her, pulsing with her breathing. Her eyes followed me as I edged toward a chair.

"We been waiting for you," Mr. Short said. "Did you bring the goat?" He was speaking to me but looking at Mr. John Barrow.

"Goat belongs to Pinch," Mr. John Barrow said, speaking to him but looking at me.

"No matter," said Mrs. Long. "John, sit close to me." She beckoned to him and he sat. "Give me your left hand. I will tell you things you could never imagine."

He took off his hat and plopped it in his lap. He gave her a big smile, giggling, and shook his head.

"Come, now, John, this won't hurt a bit. Surely you don't mind if I hold your hand?"

He lifted his hand slowly and offered it to her.

She cuddled his big, bony hand palm up.

"Oh, John, what a heart line. The ladies must drop at your feet!"

He bent his skinny head over quick.

"Where you see that?" he asked.

"And this! You are destined to be rich!"

"Where you see that?" He poked his nose close to take a look.

"Oh, my," she said suddenly. She gave his hand a squeeze.

"What you see now?"

"This!" She poked his hand with a dainty finger. "And this!" She poked again. "Those lines indicate fate and wisdom. You have both."

I stood up to take a look. It wasn't the cleanest hand I ever saw. The lines in the middle formed a big, wiggly M. I knew what that stood for. M is for mean. I looked down at my own hand. It was pretty much the same only smaller and cleaner.

"When were you born, John?" Mrs. Long asked.

"Long time ago," he said.

"Dummy," said Mr. Short. "Tell the lady your birth date."

"Last day in October," he told them.

Mrs. Long looked quickly at Mr. Short.

"Ah," she said, "I should have known. A Halloween Child. I haven't chatted with a Halloween Child in years. Will you help me, John?"

He looked puzzled. "Well," he said, "I was born on Halloween, all right." He scratched his skinny head. "I'd be pleased to help out if I knew what it is I got to do."

"John, a Halloween Child can talk to spirits and see into the future. Can you do either of those things?"

"Why, I never did 'em in my life!" He was mighty upset. "I don't want to even think on it! It's a terrible thing being a Halloween Child. I ain't going to like it at all." He stood still, puzzled. He did some more scratching, then looked hopefully at Mrs. Long.

"Probably not everybody that's born on Halloween can do those things, you think? So maybe I got nothing to worry about?"

She laid his hand down on the table.

"I wouldn't count on it, John," she said.

· 17 ·

Questions

There was a scraping kind of knock at the door and Mr. Short walked over to see who it was. He came back leading two of the sorriest people I ever saw in my life. The one in front was a big, strapping fellow dressed practically in rags. He had dirt all over him like he'd been digging graves.

The one following him was small and thin and gray-looking, with dark splotches showing where his eyes were supposed to be. Even his clothes were a kind of smooth gray color. It was like he was living only in the shadows of that flickering light.

Mr. Short ushered them to the chairs on the other side of the table from us. Mrs. Long smiled and nodded.

"Mr. John Barrow here is possibly a Halloween Child," she said.

Gray eyes swung to Mr. John Barrow and stayed there. It was so quiet you could hear the faucet dripping in the kitchen.

"Now," Mrs. Long said, "let's get started. When Mr. Short and I learned just how bad things really were here in Four Corners, we decided to stay awhile and see what we could do to help out. That's the kind of people we are. Too bad you didn't bring the goat, Pinch." She looked at me, then shifted to Mr. John Barrow.

"John, maybe you can help."

He hopped up from his chair.

"I don't have a single penny to loan nobody," he said.

"Sit down, John," Mr. Short said sharply. "Nobody wants the money you got hid. She just wants to ask you some questions."

Everybody in the room stared at Mr. John Barrow. The staring lasted a long time. Finally he sat back down.

"I heard there's a chance the Widow Adriean Barrouquere will be getting married shortly and moving away," Mrs. Long said.

"Mmmmmmm . . ." came a voice from the shadows. It was the Blotchy-eyed One.

And the Gravedigger smiled and nodded his head like he had heard all about it a long time ago and had an invitation to the wedding right in his pocket.

"And that she's got a sackful of jewels she'll bring with her," Mrs. Long said.

Silence.

"What do you say about that, John?"

Blotchy Eyes and Gravedigger fixed their eyes on Mr. John Barrow, waiting for an answer.

A big smile popped on Mr. John Barrow's face.

"Monkey married the baboon's sister, smacked his lips and then he kissed her," he sang.

He looked at all the faces, but nobody else was smiling.

"You haven't Been Told Anything, have you, John?" Mrs. Long asked.

"No ma'am," he said. "To tell the absolute truth, I ain't never heard of the lady."

"Oh," said Mrs. Long and she looked a little unhappy about that. Then she gave another try at putting some life into her party, but I could've told her it wouldn't work, 'cause this was a pretty dead bunch.

"People say Grandpa Peter Perkins is looking mighty poorly. They don't guess he'll make it to the new year."

And the Blotchy-eyed One said: "Mmmmmmm . . ."

And the Gravedigger was half grinning and nodding so hard you'd think Grandpa Perkins had already talked to him about how deep he wanted to be put.

"He probably buried all his money in an iron pot out in the swamp somewhere," Mrs. Long said.

Then, looking at nobody in particular, she asked: "Do you know where he buried the money, John?"

All those gray heads turned on him again. I truly felt sorry for Mr. John Barrow 'cause I didn't expect he would have an answer that would fit this question either.

"I had an old mule that went blind. He ran away and is probably stone-dead by now." He thought about his mule for a couple of seconds, then he said slow and serious: "You know, I ain't had a chance to talk about this kind of deep subject in a long time. It's been on my mind to ask. You think Grandpa Perkins and that old mule will end up in the same place?"

Right then I felt pretty proud of Mr. John Barrow. He had those grown-ups properly stumped. But all the attention got to him 'cause then he started to spit out steam like a teakettle. He told them about his chickens and about his twenty acres, and he even got around to his maw and paw. But I could tell they weren't really interested. The only time they even perked up was when Mrs. Long would sneak in a question.

"There was no topping my paw for being wise," Mr. John Barrow said. "He knew almost everything there was to know about most things."

And Mrs. Long asked: "Did he ever talk to you about life after death?"

And Mr. John Barrow said: "Well, once he told me about chopping off an old chicken's head, and that chicken ran around the yard for about a mile before it laid down and died." That started him back on chickens.

When Mrs. Long got her chance, she asked more

questions about buried treasure and people dying
and other creepy things, but you could see she was
getting weary of the whole thing.

◎ 18 ◎

Séance

"Well, John, that's that. You're certainly no Halloween Child. You don't know a single thing about
the future or about where people are hiding things or
anything really important, do you?" She let the question dangle there.

He scratched some. "That ain't true."

"Well, then?"

"I know where some mighty fine furs are hid."

"Mr. John Barrow!" I yelled.

Mr. Short glanced at Mrs. Long. She smiled and
nodded. Then she reached over and picked up Mr.
John Barrow's skinny hand again. She stroked it.
Suddenly her head bowed, her chin rested on her
chest. Her breathing became heavy.

I wanted to yell at Mr. John Barrow again.

Mrs. Long's right eye opened. It stared at the table

in front of her. Then it moved up, searching the room. It lit on me and stayed there.

I tingled. My skin tightened. My bones pulled closer together. I didn't want anything slithering in my pores or between my bones. I rolled up tighter than a doodlebug, waiting to see what was going to happen.

The room got colder. There was a fuzz in my mind. It was like I was falling asleep.

"Are you all right, my dear?" Mr. Short asked her in a whisper I could barely hear.

No sound. Only breathing. Then a voice.

"Mr. John Barrow!"

It was a deep voice, the voice of a man. But it seemed to be coming out of Mrs. Long. Her head raised ever so slightly as the voice spoke, but not enough to see her lips. Then her head dropped back to her chest. I looked through the fuzz at Mr. John Barrow.

He sat there, tense, staring at her, eyes as narrow as buttonholes. It was like he was watching a wild animal sitting on a tree limb, praying it wouldn't leap his way.

"Mr. John Barrow!" the voice demanded again.

He stood up slowly. "What?" he asked angrily. He used both hands to push himself up from the table. I stopped looking at his face and started watching those long, skinny fingers. The fingers were twitching. The nails were scratching holes into the wood tabletop. He was past being scared. He was like a muskrat backed into a shallow hole, ready to claw his way out.

"Calm down, now, John. Nobody's going to get hurt," Mr. Short said sharply.

Mr. John Barrow stood silent for a moment, staring at Mrs. Long. When he spoke, his voice had lost some of its anger. It trembled. There was fear in it.

"I don't like what's happening here!"

"John!" the deep voice spoke to him again.

"What!" The anger was back and the fingers clawed at the table.

"Your father wants to talk to you."

I looked quick from Mrs. Long to Mr. John Barrow. He sat down very slowly, hands still fixed on the tabletop. He didn't say a word.

Mr. John Barrow's paw had been a big man who farmed a little, same as him, but was probably better at it. He says his paw was a stern man, but a good one. Liked to belt his bottom when he got into trouble. He is full of stories about having some fun and ending up getting his bottom belted. But I never heard him say a cross word about his paw.

"You listening?" the voice asked him.

Mr. John Barrow nodded. "Could I say something?" he asked. A slow nod from Mrs. Long.

"Hello, Paw." He kind of smiled.

"Hello, John."

"I been behaving myself, Paw. Farm's in pretty good shape. Roof don't leak too bad. Good crop of sweet potatoes. Been keeping the weeds off your grave, but I guess you noticed. And I got a yard full of chickens, case you want to stay for dinner."

"Shut up, John," the deep voice said.

"Old mule went blind and ran away, Paw. Got to git a new one."

"Shut up, John."

He shut up.

There was a noise outside the window. My head jerked around. The window shades were closed tight, but there was a rip in one of them and I could see into the side yard. It was bright outside. There was something on the ground. Heavy. Large. Gray. A mockingbird. Biggest mockingbird I ever saw. It stood perfectly still and stared at the house. Then its large beak opened wide.

"We got to help these folks solve the problem, John."

"All right, Paw."

I kept watching the mockingbird. It stared silently at the house. Then its beak opened again.

"Where are they hiding all those furs, John?"

"Mr. John Barrow!" I yelled at him. But my jaws locked and my tongue swelled and filled my whole mouth and no sound came out.

He wasn't tense any longer. He was talking to his paw like it was something he did every day. His face was peaceful. It was kind of like he was someplace else.

"In the loft of the Judge's barn," he said.

I couldn't move to stop him.

"What's that?" Mr. Short asked loudly.

"Thank you, John," the deep voice said.

The mockingbird lifted its wings and flew away.

"Paw, did I tell you what I'm going to name the new mule? I'm going to name him after Uncle Fred Fulkerson. Paw?"

"He's gone, John," Mr. Short told him and stood up.

My mind was clearing. Somebody pushed back a chair and I heard the scrape on the wood floor. Things were almost back to normal. Mrs. Long's eyes were still closed. Then her head lifted. Her eyes opened slowly. She sat upright. A bright smile came on her face. Mr. Short put his arm around her shoulder.

"How did it go?" she asked.

"We got all we need," he answered.

She stood up and they walked toward the door.

That's when I yelled at him.

"Who stole our furs from you? And what do you know about my baby goats?" He turned and stared at me.

"Don't know a thing about any goats, boy, and those furs weren't exactly yours. We traded. Remember?"

"You traded with Mr. John Barrow, not me and Charley."

"No matter. They are gone now."

"Who stole them from you?"

"Can't say for sure," he said. "But I can tell you one thing. You see a big, tall skinny fellow wearing a white hat, you watch out for him."

He opened the door and they were gone.

◉ 19 ◉

Graveyard Talk

I ran all the way home.

"Dad?"

He was sitting on the front steps, staring into space.

"What now!" He turned his eyes on me.

"The little people know all about the furs you got stashed away in the Judge's barn."

"HOW'D THEY FIND THAT OUT!"

"Mr. John Barrow kind of let it slip out."

"Ho-lee-gee!"

He looked around for another muskrat trap to slam against a tree, but his eyes lit on the one he had already smashed to smithereens and that stopped him.

"Oh, boy!" he said. "All right, I pretty much got hold of myself now. I was sitting on the porch thinking, but it's past time for thinking. The muskrat war has been declared. Pinch, I'm going to ask some of the men to help. You go find that skinny gray fellow who says he's a lawman and tell him to meet us at the store. If you see the Judge, tell him we want him too. Chances are you won't find him.

"And, Pinch," his voice softened, "go tell Ben Riedlinger I'd be pleased if he could make it too." And off he went.

Suddenly, I didn't know what to do. Mr. Short said a tall, skinny fellow in a white hat had stolen the furs. Cat Eyes O'Toole had been wearing an almost-white hat when he said he was chasing two little people to put them in jail.

I went inside. Mom was taking a nap. I walked quiet so I wouldn't wake her up. Then I did something I never did before. I took Dad's twenty-two out of the closet, loaded it, and walked out the back door trembling every step. I didn't ask. I just did it.

Partway down the road toward the Judge's house a crow saw me coming and called a warning. I shivered. The crow never showed itself. The rest of the way it was quiet. But I didn't feel right.

He was standing in the cornfield, skinnier and grayer-looking than I remembered. But I knew it was him by the almost-white hat. My eyes blinked a bare second. When I looked again, he wasn't there. I searched the weeds and cornstalks back and forth. Then I spotted the hat. He had stooped down, maybe hiding. He was right beside a large block of stone.

What to do? I waited in the road. He stood up, spotted me and waved, then knelt down again.

I wasn't keen on breaking up that man's prayers. When I got closer I saw a pail of water resting on top of the big stone.

Next to the pail was a straight razor with a bright-red handle.

"My dad is going after the little people and he asks your help."

He straightened up.

"Does he know where they are?"

"He's probably going to start looking at the Judge's barn."

He splashed water on his gray face and it dripped down his skinny chin and on his shirt. Then he smiled. A mean man couldn't smile so good. I smiled back and a little bit of the fear slipped away.

"Never saw a razor with a red handle before," I told him.

"It's nice, isn't it?" He reached over and picked it up. He flicked the blade open. It was bright. It bounced the sunrays as his hand moved. The edge was sharp enough to slit a hog's throat. Suddenly he wasn't smiling any more, and his dark eyes stared at me.

"Don't move a muscle," he hissed. I froze. "Now, turn your head very slowly to the left."

It was a tingly time. It was broad daylight. He stood there, holding a gleaming razor with a blood-red handle. He wanted me to turn my head away from him.

I moved my eyes, but my grip tightened on my rifle. There was nothing to see but grass and trees. I moved my head. I stared straight across my shoulder. Then I saw it.

A white-tailed deer stood at the edge of the trees, watching us. The tines on the left antler were broken off close to the beam. The deer's head tilted sideways.

"Don't make a noise, now."

I wasn't about to. My dad trained me pretty good as a hunter. My body was lined up perfect for a shot. I moved the rifle slowly upward toward my shoulder.

"Son, I wish you wouldn't shoot." He said it soft and slow. "That deer comes here every morning. It's a kind of visit. I've got an apple in my pocket for him, and he is waiting for us to leave so he can come and get it."

Deer is food. Venison is tasty to eat. I never heard of anybody who fed apples to deer. I lowered the rifle.

"Pinch, why don't you just sit down on the ground and we can talk till I finish here. That flop-headed deer won't move a muscle unless he hears the welkin ring." His voice stayed soft. He returned to his shaving.

"What's a welkin ring?"

"You know how to read?"

"I do."

"Then look it up."

"That's what the schoolteacher is always saying."

"Well, she is right. Glad you stopped by, Pinch. I been hoping for a chance to talk to you. The Judge says you are a strong-headed boy. I can see he is right. I admire that in a boy."

We talked. I told him about the muskrat furs and the sack of dog fur.

"Shame you lost your furs," he said, scraping whiskers off his face.

I was starting to like the idea of having him help. He had a strong, clear voice and it sounded like he could take care of himself. Even out in the sunlight he still had a gray look, but when he talked his eyes smiled. And he was nice to the deer.

I looked over to where the deer was grazing. It wasn't paying any attention to us. I wondered if you could really bait a deer with an apple and then shoot it. Seems like there would be something unfair about that. I didn't feel the same way about baiting a muskrat trap. Maybe the bad feeling only starts when the animal is big enough to stare you straight in the eye.

He finished shaving, splashed more water in his face, then dried and folded his red-handled razor.

"Where did you get the razor?"

He unfolded the razor, took careful hold of the blade, and thrust the red handle at me.

"Take a look," he said. "My grandpa here gave it to me." He patted the big stone. "Grandpa O'Toole was born in a house that sat on this very piece of ground. He lived a full life back home, but he wanted to be buried where he was born, and that's why he's buried under this here dirt. First time I saw him use the red-handled razor I was about your age. I got him to put shaving soap all over my face. I scratched it off with the handle of my toothbrush." He stopped talking and thought about it.

"Then one day he gave me the razor. It was kind of a prize." He took back the razor, folded it closed, and put it in his pocket.

"I'll tell you how it happened, Pinch. When I was a boy I had a friend who used to cheat me all the time. One day he traded me a baby raccoon for a puppy dog. Never cuddled a raccoon before. I thought I'd made the best trade of my life. But he didn't tell me the raccoon couldn't live without its mother. It died before it lived a week. First I thought it was my fault. But Grandpa told me I got cheated again. I was so mad I told Grandpa I would never trade with that boy again. That's when he gave me the red razor. He said a man really gets to be a man when he realizes you can't trust nobody. Even people you think are pretty nice." He picked up the water pail and threw the water out.

"You think on that, Pinch. It's kind of a warning I'm giving you. Now, let's go drop the water pail off at the Judge's house."

I stood up. The deer saw the movement and fixed its eyes on us again. I suddenly felt the smoothness of the wood on the rifle stock. I would remember that flop-headed deer standing there watching us every time I went hunting for the rest of my life.

Cat Eyes reached in his pocket and pulled out the red apple. There was a wet spot on top of the headstone where the water pail had sat. He put the apple right in the center of the wet spot. By the time we reached the other side of the field, the deer had begun walking toward the apple.

We dropped the bucket off at the Judge's. You could see the big red barn from where we stood near the front gate.

"Son," Cat Eyes said, "you go on home. Tell your dad I'll be there pretty soon. I got some things I want to do first."

◉ 20 ◉

The Trapping Pool

Most of the men were already sitting on the store porch when I got back. Mr. Ben Riedlinger and Charley were over on one end all by themselves.

I told Dad that Cat Eyes would be along later. He nodded and motioned the men around him.

Right then Mom called me inside and I didn't get to hear one word of what he was going to say.

"Pinch," Mom said, "I know you'd rather be out there with the men, but I need your help with the

• 94 •

dishes. And just 'cause you are in a hurry is no excuse for doing a poor job."

"You know what's happening over there?"

"I do, and I'll tell you something you don't know if you will just slow down. Can't afford to have you break a dish, Pinch."

I picked up a soup bowl and wiped it off so careful you'd of thought it was fine china. Truth is, we bought it from the store about a year ago for a quarter.

"Well," Mom said, "you probably ought not mention to your dad what I tell you, but in a way you are responsible for what's happening at the meeting. Him and me talked about it today. He said he's tired of bickering with Ben Riedlinger. He said he couldn't really fault a man trying to feed his family. Said he wanted to put it right, but didn't know how to do it." She had finished with the dishes and was washing out the sink.

"That's when I reminded him that you and Charley and John had landed on the answer weeks ago." She handed me a dry glass. "Go put this glass in the china closet, Pinch."

I wasn't sure what she was getting at. I went into the front room to put the glass away and took a peek out the window while I was there. Charley was sitting on the steps, head tilted back, taking it all in. I hurried back to finish the dishes.

"You three decided to band together and share what you trapped. The idea of sharing was a good one. You just didn't watch John Barrow close enough, that's all. Your dad gave what you did some thought and figured he might be able to make use of the good parts."

I stuck the last dish in the cupboard.

"Can I go now?"

"On your marks," she said.

Dad was still talking. "The Judge was supposed to be here to make it legal, but he ain't. But every man here is as good as his word. We pool what we catch. Each man's profit depends on how many traps he has. We get a better price for having a lot of furs to sell at one time. And Tony gets a share for keeping the books and dealing with the buyers. We take our share back in cash or store goods. Everybody agree to that?" There was nodding all around.

"Mr. Grimball?"

"What you want, Henry Sweet?"

"Does skunks count?"

That's the kind of question you'd expect from Henry. Him and his brother Billy are grown men, but they don't often act like it. I mean, they don't do a stick of work unless they have to. They spend most of their time fishing and they don't even know where the fish are biting. The two of them are more likely to get caught in their own traps.

"Skunks are selling pretty good, Henry, so I guess they count," Dad said. "Now, let's move out. I got my furs stored in the Judge's barn, so let's start there. And if we meet those little people on the way, we'll find out what they know. Then we'll give them a fair trial and throw them in jail."

Everybody stood up and stretched. Dad looked straight at Mr. Ben Riedlinger. He walked over to him and stuck out his hand. The two of them shook pretty good. All the men began laughing and shaking each other's hands.

I looked over at Charley. For the first time he looked back at me.

"Hey, Charley, I got two nickels. You want a root beer?"

He hopped up the porch stairs, a big grin on his face. We strutted inside the door and I plunked my two nickels down on the counter in front of Mrs. Nell.

The root beer went down cold and sweet.

"Pretty good-tasting root beer," I told him. He plopped his empty bottle down on the counter.

"Ain't too bad," said my friend Charley.

◉ **21** ◉

The Foreigner

When the men got to the barn, Dad rushed inside to check out the loft. He came out smiling.

"Somebody's been messing with the lock on the door to the loft, but it's still O.K. Chicken feathers and eaten-on chicken bones everywhere. Our missing chickens been keeping the little people fat."

Mr. Short's wagon was sitting outside the barn, empty except for a couple of burlap sacks and some chopped firewood.

"Henry Sweet, you check out that wagon," my dad yelled.

Henry went over and untied one of the sacks and looked inside. He stared a long time. He tied it back up. He untied the other one and looked inside.

"Just hides," he yelled, and retied it.

"Well, you and Billy haul them inside the barn afore somebody steals them. And maybe you better haul the firewood in too. We are going to wait them out and maybe we'll want a fire."

We went inside the barn to look. There was a soft noise behind the tool-shed door. Dad put his finger to his lips and walked over to the door without making a sound. He took hold of the handle and jerked it open.

"Grrrrr!" The dog leaped. Sharp teeth snapped. Dad jerked his arm away and I heard cloth rip. Dad slammed the door shut and the dog crashed into it.

"Did he get you?" I ran over. A part of Dad's sleeve had been ripped away.

"I'm O.K., Pinch, but he nearly bit my arm off." He pushed the wooden latch into place. The dog was suddenly silent.

"Pinch, you let everybody know what's locked up in here. We'll figure out what to do with this dog later."

The men sat and waited for hours. Then Mr. Tony said his store needed tending to and he had to go home. Mr. John Barrow said it was way past lunch-time and he was mighty hungry. Somebody else said his feet hurt and he had to go home and soak them. The Sweets had already gone home without telling a soul.

"Wait a minute!" Dad said. "We won't be finished until we get our hands on that little man. You go on home and eat a bite or soak your feet or whatever, then come on back. All right?"

The men nodded and grinned and headed for home.

"I ain't going no place," said Mr. Ben Ried-linger. He stood there, his strong hand curled around his rifle. Dad smiled. He had an army of one. That was all he needed.

"Pinch," Dad said, "you boys run home and tell your mothers what's going on. Then bring us back something tasty to eat." He turned to Mr. Riedlinger. "That all right with you?"

"That's all right with me, Will."

But my mom didn't like the idea at all.

"You tell your father I ain't one bit happy about being by myself all day long. Too many strange things going on. Suppose somebody knocks on the door. Don't he care what happens to me?" But she packed some food and said the weather was getting colder by the minute and I should tell Dad he better not come home with a sniffly nose.

When we got back to the red barn, there wasn't a sound. The two men sat near the barn entrance. We moved inside, found a spot to sit, and unwrapped our supper.

"You want some of this fried chicken, Will?"

"Thank you, Ben. How about you taking one of these biscuits?"

There was silence while we chewed. I'd of taken a piece of that spicy chicken too, but nobody offered.

"What was that?" Dad asked suddenly. He hopped up and ran on tiptoe to the barn door. But there weren't any other sounds. He came back, leaned over, and whispered something to Mr. Ben Riedlinger. Then he sat down again and finished chewing.

"It's getting cold in here," Dad said, putting down a chicken bone. "Pinch, you and Charley close the barn doors. We going to need a fire."

The minute the cold wind couldn't freeze our tails I started getting warmer. Rich people like the Judge have pretty good barns.

"I'll build the fire," Mr. Ben Riedlinger said.

"Ben, I wouldn't mind doing that," Dad said. He swept a place clean on the dirt floor.

Pretty soon flame hopped up and I scrambled close to get the chill out of my bones.

"Ben, you want to sit here on this stool?"

"That's all right, Will. This piece of log will do fine."

They were trying to out-nice one another, is what they were doing. The fighting was over but they hadn't settled back to their regular ways. It was quiet while everybody was getting warm.

"Will, you remember the last time you and me carried a gun planning to shoot something bigger than a squirrel? Think I should tell the boys?"

The two men looked at one another, but for a while not another word was said. Then Mr. Ben Riedlinger stood up and stretched. He walked around a little bit on his gimp leg.

"Will and me weren't more than kids ourselves. We got on a ship and sailed off to war. Something was watching over the two of us, 'cause the very day we got to the front lines was the day the fighting ended. An old sergeant with his arm in a sling took one look at us and told us to get on back where we come from. We had walked twenty miles that day. Now we had to walk twenty miles back." He looked over at my dad like he was asking if he should talk some more. Dad stared into the fire.

"It was a mighty hot day. When we heard a spring flowing we left the road and cut into the woods. When we got to the spring, there was a foreigner stooping down on the other side, dipping his hat in the water.

"He must've sensed something 'cause suddenly his head popped up. He stared at us. The water drained from his hat. We stared back. We were holding our rifles loose. His own rifle leaned against a tree about ten feet back from the stream.

"Well, we knew the war was over. The stream had plenty of water for everybody. We nodded to him and drank our fill. Then we nodded again, turned our backs, and headed for the road.

"The rifle cracked before we had walked three steps. My legs fell out from under me. Wasn't any pain. I just smacked the ground. Will here dove for the bushes, pulled his rifle to his shoulder, and put a bullet between the foreigner's eyes before he even had a chance to get off a second shot."

There was a long silence. Then my dad started talking very slowly.

"I can still remember the quiet," he said. "I was laying there thinking that two men are dead 'cause one of them hadn't heard the war was over." He stood up and poked at the fire. "Then Ben stirred and said a cuss word and I knew my friend was going to live to hunt squirrels again another day."

◉ 22 ◉

Target Practice

The barn was getting cold again.

"What's happening around here?" Dad said sharply, staring at the fire. "That little man has started a muskrat war in Four Corners. Me and Ben been fighting. We never did that before. Charley and Pinch been fighting. You boys fight some, but not too much. Four Corners was already having its problems. That little man brought us one problem too many. I tell you, I'm thinking hard about shooting that man. Maybe the muskrat war is about over. But if a little man gets killed, it won't bother me a bit."

I watched my dad. Something was happening that I didn't understand. For one thing, I knew he wanted those skins back and he wanted to boot the little people out of Four Corners. But killing people just wasn't his way. And something else. His words were strong and hard, but there was a little smile on his face.

"One thing we got to do for sure, Ben."

"What's that?"

"We got to kill that dog."

"Right."

"Maybe drown it."

"Right."

"Or just shoot it."

"Right."

"First thing in the morning."

"Right."

They kept smiling. Then Dad stood up, shaking his head side to side.

"Ben, we been having so much fun I almost forgot I got to run my trapline. You and the boys watch over things here. Then bring *everybody* to Tony's."

After he left, Mr. Ben Riedlinger sat there, still smiling.

"Nothing to do around here. Maybe I ought to get in a little dog-shooting target practice. You boys see any good targets around here?"

I never heard a grown man talking so silly. Now he was going to shoot a rifle inside a closed barn.

"It's dark in here," I told him.

"Pinch, you do me a favor. Pick up the lantern and walk over there by the door. Maybe we will find something. I'll load this rifle and get ready."

I did what he told me. But I don't like walking with my back to loaded rifles. He was carrying a thirty-thirty, and even if it missed me it was going to tear a huge hole in the side of the Judge's barn.

"Stop right about there, Pinch. See them sacks of hides that Henry brought in from outside? Set the lantern right beside them and come back here." I did what he told me, wondering.

"Now, boys, I'm going to show you some fancy shooting. I'll close one eye and shoot the tie ropes clean off those two sacks. I don't want to blow too big a hole in the furs, so I'll aim careful with my one open eye." He raised the rifle.

"Charley, you want to count to three?"

"One!" Charley said. I heard a rustling sound.

"Two!" Shadows from the lantern light danced on the sacks of muskrat fur. I heard the click as he cocked the rifle.

"STOP!" shouted one of the sacks of muskrat fur.

"PLEASE!" shouted the other sack.

I looked at Mr. Ben Riedlinger. His eyes were twinkling. There was a big grin on his face.

"Got 'em!" he shouted.

Suddenly a knife ripped through one of the sacks and a little head poked out. When Mr. Short saw Mr. Ben Riedlinger smiling at him, he started shouting.

"Get me out of here! I am frozen stiff. I've been smelling fried chicken for hours and my stomach is grumbling. My arms and legs are cramped and lifeless. I have never suffered so much in my entire life!"

Mr. Ben Riedlinger went over and took the knife away from him and pulled him out of the sack. Then he opened the other sack and helped Mrs. Long out.

"I must get to that fire immediately," she pleaded. Her words shook with her shivering.

Mr. Ben Riedlinger let them warm up by the fire. Then we opened the barn doors, stomped out the fire, and set out. There wasn't much talking on the way to Mr. Tony's. Only two questions the whole way, and neither one of them got helpful answers.

About halfway, Mr. Short stopped, rubbed his little hands together, and turned to Mr. Ben Riedlinger.

"You really going to shoot my dog?"

"Never killed a dog in my life," he answered. "Never even thought about doing it until now."

He prodded Mr. Short with the rifle, telling him to get moving. I watched as they walked ahead. Mr. Ben Riedlinger moved pretty good on his gimp leg. That reminded me of a question of my own. I ran to catch up.

"Was what you told us about my dad shooting that foreigner between the eyes a true story?"

He looked down at me and smiled.

"Pinch," he said, "every word in that story is almost true."

⊙ 23 ⊙

Jury

Mr. Tony Carmouche was sitting on his front porch, rocking and waiting, when we got there.

"Where'd you find them?" he called to us.

"Sniffing around Judge Boudreaux's barn. From the smell of them, they been sleeping there for a couple of nights."

"Where's your dad, Pinch?" Mr. Tony asked.

"He's walking traps," I told him. "Said he would be here as soon as he could."

Mr. Tony stood up and walked toward us. Today was his day for deputy-sheriffing 'cause he had his badge pinned on his shirt. Even without the badge, you could've seen it in his walk. He's a short-legged man, and he's got a short-legged walk. But when the law is involved, he has a kind of side-to-side motion to his walk like a cowman fresh off a horse. He probably learned it at the movies.

"Anybody seen the Sweet boys?" Mr. Ben Riedlinger asked. Mr. Tony shook his head. "Well, they helped these little people hide in the sacks, so we are gonna have to round them up."

Wasn't another word spoken until we were almost to the porch and Mrs. Long stepped in a puddle of muddy water.

"Oh, dear, first we are rounded up like common criminals and now these adorable shoes are soggy wet and will certainly shrink." She glanced at Mr. Ben Riedlinger, but he moved his gun up toward his shoulder, so she didn't slow down any.

"I want you two to know I'm here to make sure you get a fair trial," Mr. Tony told the little people.

"Trial! In the middle of the swamp!" Mr. Short planted his small feet in the ground and wouldn't budge one step farther.

"You don't have to worry," Mr. Tony told him. "This here trial will be presided over by Judge Ridley Boudreaux, and there ain't no man in Four Corners who knows the law better, or who is fairer to polecats who break it."

Mr. Short took Mrs. Long by the arm and the two of them started forward again.

"I want to see the Judge! Right now! I've already got a long list of complaints about this *creature* marching us around with a gun at our backs." He nodded back at Mr. Ben Riedlinger, but if Mr. Ben Riedlinger minded he didn't let on.

"Well, the Judge ain't exactly here yet, but he's coming." Mr. Tony turned to me. "Pinch, why ain't

your paw here yet? I want to get this trial started."
He turned around and walked inside, not waiting for
an answer.

When we got inside, practically the whole town was
sitting in the dining room around a big table. Mr.
Tony walked to the head of the table and sat down,
drumming his fingers to make sure everybody knew
he was in a hurry to get started. There was an empty
chair for the Judge.

"You two sit right over there so you will be across
from the Judge when he gets here," Mr. Tony told
the prisoners. "Rest of you, find a seat. We are going
to get started."

Mr. Short held the chair for Mrs. Long, then slid
it forward daintily. You could tell he wasn't from
Four Corners.

"Do I understand that you are going to start a
trial of two perfectly innocent people without even
having the decency to wait for the Judge?"

"We will save talk of innocence until this particular trial is over," Mr. Tony said.

Mr. Short's eyes roamed around the dark room.

"Can't hardly see in here, but I see one thing loud
and clear. Can't have a trial without a jury, and you
certainly don't have a jury here, unless you have it
hidden in the darker corners of this room."

"All we need is twelve," said Mr. Tony. "You can
count 'em for yourself. There's me and Nell and
Ben and his missus and Victoria and Pinch and
Charley."

"That's only seven! And two of them are children!"

"Children got rights, same as everybody else. Especially, children who had their property stolen like Pinch and Charley here."

"Traded, not stolen. It was a legitimate trade. And if this is going to be a legitimate jury, you are still five short."

"Tony?" Mr. John Barrow called, holding up his hand.

"Hold on, John." He turned to Mr. Short. "Will Grimball and that O'Toole fellow will be here in a minute."

"That still leaves you three short."

"Tony?" Mr. John Barrow said.

"One minute, John. We got to get this settled." He turned back to Mr. Short, smiling. "This is going to be a fairer trial than most, 'cause we decided that we would let you sit on your own jury. You each get a vote. You want to cast it now, or you want to wait?"

"Tony?"

"All right now, John, what you got on your mind?"

"Jist letting you know I'm here, Tony."

"I know you're here, John. I'm looking right at you."

"But you ain't counting me in on the jury."

"Oh."

Mr. Tony Carmouche looked puzzled for a minute. Then he turned to Mr. Short.

"You see there? We got twelve people on this here

jury. That enough for you?" He turned back to Mr. John Barrow and gave him a little nod. Then he knocked his fist on the table and stood up.

"I'm calling this court in session for Judge Ridley Boudreaux. Let's have some quiet. I thought we'd get started by letting these accused people tell us what they are guilty of and why they did what they did. You can both talk, or only one. Suit yourselves. But no standing up, and no shouting." He sat down. With a wave of his hand, he turned the speaking over to the two little people.

Mr. Short stared at him. Wasn't any doubt he was heading for a long stay in jail, but he didn't look worried one bit

◎ 24 ◎

Trial

"This lovely lady and myself are guilty of nothing. A few simple trades with kind townspeople along the bayou, nothing more." Mr. Short stared at Mr. Tony.

"That's your defense?"

"It's the truth!"

Mr. Tony stuck his hand in his pocket, pulled out a long piece of paper and held it up, showing it all around.

"This here's a list of maybe twenty people, up the bayou, down the bayou, wherever. All of them claim that a little man and a little woman stopped by their house, talked long and pretty, and went away with good furs, leaving bad furs behind."

Mr. Short popped to his feet. "Only a man who doesn't know his furs would say that the Catahoula fur was anything less than first-class!"

"First-class dog!" Charley shouted.

Mr. Tony stared at Charley, telling him with a hard look to be quiet.

"Certainly, this child is no judge of fine furs? I understand that Mr. Grimball is an expert trapper. Did he see the furs?"

"No."

"Well, who did? This *creature* with the rifle?" He pointed to Mr. Ben Riedlinger.

"Me," said Mr. Tony.

"The deputy sheriff? You trap animals as well as men?"

"I ain't much on trapping," he said, "but I'm pretty good on dogs."

Mr. Tony started drumming his fingers on the table again. Things were moving too slow for him.

"We'll fetch the furs in a minute and me and Ben can examine them. Anybody know where they are?"

I did. Mr. John Barrow had sewed them together

and made a blanket, like Mr. Tony said to do. But the smell was so bad, he hadn't gotten around to using it yet.

"John, you go get the blanket," Mr. Tony told him.

"Tony, I'll do it, but it ain't fair to send me now. I want to stay and see what happens."

But that wasn't what Mr. Tony wanted, so Mr. John Barrow left, slamming the door behind him.

"All right now, let's get back to business. The next thing we got to talk about is how you been fleecing trappers for miles around, making them pay hard-earned money to trap on railroad land. Except that the railroad ain't collecting for trapping on their land. Least I don't think they are. Now what you got to say about that?"

Mr. Short hopped to his feet. He pounded his little fist on the table.

"It's bad enough you twisting and turning the things we do into crimes," he shouted. "Every single man we traded with could be rich by now if he had half the sense he ought to. *Now* you are accusing us of crimes we certainly did not commit. I say sir, did *not* commit!"

Bang! went his little fist. He stared at Mr. Tony, waiting for him to say something.

"I say sir, what evidence do you have?"

Then I heard the front door open and Dad walked into the dining room. He stood in the doorway, peering into the dim light, nodding when he saw a familar face, staring a bit longer when the face was unfamiliar. When he got to Mr. Short he looked a long, long time. Mr. Short stared back.

"Sit down, Will. We've already started, but it's your turn. Maybe you got something to say to Mr. Short here."

Dad walked to a chair where he could get a clearer look at the little people. He sat. He looked.

"This ain't the railroad man," he said.

"What?"

"It was a little man, but not this little. About up to here." He held his hand about his shoulder height off the floor. "And I found out he really was from the railroad."

Mr Short and Mrs. Long were smiling again. It was a confident smile.

"What did I tell you," Mr. Short said. "Innocent again. Always innocent. Always trying to do good for people. Always accused of evildoing. But innocent nonetheless."

"Will Grimball, you sure?" Mr. Tony scratched the back of his neck. Things were getting complicated.

"Not a doubt. But that don't end things. What about my goat? Somebody kidnapped my goat and stole her kids. What you got to say about that?"

Mr. Short sat there, kind of smirking.

"Mr. Grimball, I don't know a single thing about your goat. Or anybody's goat. And I want to ask you a question of my own. Did you personally see those fine

Catahoula furs I traded your boy for a few paltry muskrat skins?" He waited for an answer, chin stuck out front.

Dad shook his head.

"Then how is it that we stand accused?" He turned again to Mrs. Long. "I believe it is time for us to be on our way."

"We ain't talked about the chicken stealing yet," said Mr. Ben Riedlinger. He stood just behind them, the rifle still hanging loose, but there wasn't a doubt that he still meant business.

That was when Mr. Tony stood up.

"I don't think I'd want to punish a man with only chicken feathers as evidence. I'm beginning to think it's a good thing Judge Boudreaux didn't show up. We ain't got much of a case here, specially if that dog fur don't turn out to be dog. No proof about the goat, either. Let's just sit until John comes back. We can take a close look at those furs and decide what to do."

There was a kind of scraping knock on the front door. Slowly it swung open. Cat Eyes stood there, longer and leaner and grayer than the last time I saw him. His eyes moved slowly around the room. Then he spoke.

"I'm arresting these two little people in the name of the law," he said. His voice was soft, but it was strong.

"Wait a minute," said Mr. Tony. "I thought I was the law around here."

Cat Eyes fixed a slanty-eyed stare on him. "You got evidence to hold them on?" he asked.

"Not yet we don't."

"Well, then, I'll take them off your hands. I showed my papers. I got first claim. I been chasing this pair too long to turn them over to you. They'll get exactly what they deserve. You can count on it."

"What about my little goats they probably stole?" Dad asked.

"I'll send word back if I find out something," Cat Eyes said. "That all right with you?"

He reached in his pocket, pulled out a silver pistol about a foot long, and pointed it in the general direction of the two little people.

"You two, move," he said.

I looked at faces around the room. Mr. Tony was angry. The rest were just watching.

The three of them marched out the door and the trial was over. Something wasn't right about all this.

• 25 •

The Barn

"Pinch," Dad said the minute the door had closed, "you and Charley get on over to the barn and keep watch. Soon as I can borrow a horse and wagon, I'm getting those furs out of there. Too many people know where they are."

Charley and I ran all the way. From the road I could see the barn door was open. We moved slow and came in on the barn from the back. Couldn't see a thing. Then I heard something and dropped to my knees. Charley did the same. We listened.

"Three, four, shut the door," said a voice.

"I'll be a lot happier with 'nine, ten, a big fat hen,' " said another.

It was Billy and Henry Sweet, up to foolishness. My dad would be pleased when he found out where they were. We moved through the tall grass as quiet as we could, heading to where we could see the front of the barn. They had gone inside.

Then they came marching out of the barn, each

with a bale of muskrat furs balanced on top of his head. We watched them walk back toward the bayou. We waited, not moving. There wasn't another sound coming from the barn.

We pulled back and circled around to where we could see the boat landing. The Sweet boys had already dumped the bales and were heading back to the barn.

There was a middle-sized flatboat tied to the landing. The poles for pushing it through the bayou were leaning on a nearby tree. Maybe a dozen bales of skins were already in the boat.

"Five, six, pick up sticks," a voice yelled.

"You better shut your mouth," another voice said, getting closer. "If anybody finds out what we are doing, we won't get paid."

Me and Charley lay flat in the grass until they had unloaded again and gone back to the barn for more skins.

"Charley, we got to go back and tell our dads what's happening here. Billy and Henry are stealing the furs." But then I had an idea that would keep them here until we got back. I motioned Charley to follow me. We crept through the tall grass toward the boat landing. The boat poles were the answer. I took hold of one of the heavy poles and dragged it toward the boat. Charley saw what I was doing and grabbed the other one. We cleared away some of the bales of fur already in the boat and laid the poles flat on the deck. Then we covered them carefully with the bales. It was a fine trick. The more furs they loaded, the harder it was going to be for them to get at the poles. No poles and there wasn't a chance they could get away.

Feet-shuffling noises came from the direction of the barn. We ducked back into the grass. The Sweets passed only a dozen feet away.

"Now let's go get our dads," Charley whispered.

"But my little goats might be in that barn. They got to be somewhere."

How would we get to the barn without being seen? And where was that long-toothed dog?

⊙ **26** ⊙

Jail

The high grass would hide us until we got pretty close to the barn. There was the little toolroom right inside the door. Maybe there was an angry dog in there and maybe there wasn't. We'd have to wait and see. Next time the Sweets loaded up and walked toward the bayou, we would bolt for the toolroom. Then we would check out every corner of that barn for the little goats.

The Sweets left. I crossed my fingers. We dashed for the barn. We listened hard outside the toolroom door, but there wasn't a sound. I opened the door a crack and peeked inside. No dog. We hopped in and closed the door. We waited. Suddenly there was the sound of footsteps in the barn. Then the sound of wood slamming hard against wood.

And then a voice.

"You are in. Now let's see you get out." It was the voice of Mr. Short. "You'll stay locked up until we're well gone."

"Where's Cat Eyes O'Toole?" I yelled at him.

"Who? Oh . . . errr, we gave him the slip. Now, quiet in there."

We heard him walking away. For about five minutes there wasn't any sound. Then the Sweets came back for another load.

"Nineteen, twenty, that's half the money," Billy Sweet recited.

We could hear them climb to the loft, the mumble of conversation as they talked with Mr. Short, then the thump of two more bales being dropped to the barn floor.

"How you children doing?" It was the voice of Billy Sweet. He was standing outside the toolroom door.

"Billy Sweet, you've picked the wrong side to be on. When our dads find out, you'll be sorry."

"Better rich sorry than poor sorry," Billy said. "We getting a dollar each for this work, Pinch. And

I can use the money." The two of them moved off. About ten minutes later they were back, there was more talking with Mr. Short, more feet shuffling.

Then suddenly the toolroom door flew open. Mr. Short stood in the doorway. He had a leather strap in his hand. And he wasn't alone. Standing right behind him was the Gravedigger and the Blotchy-eyed One.

"Where are the poles?" There was an angry look on his face. But we had been in that cobwebby little toolroom for half an hour, and we had angrier looks on ours. The leather strap was for show. He wasn't big enough to strap us, even with the help of the gray people. And the world would never see the day when Billy or Henry would risk standing up to my dad after giving us a licking. We kept looking angrier back at him than he looked at us.

"The poles, the poles, where are the poles?"

"Where are the little goats?"

"Young man, let's cut out this foolishness." He smacked the leather strap hard against the door frame. "Where are the poles?"

"Where are the goats?"

"I don't have the slightest idea where your goats are!" He stomped his little foot.

There was a yelling outside, and the Sweets rushed out to see what it was, then rushed back in.

"Somebody's coming!"

When Mr. Short went out, me and Charley did the same.

"Dog! Dog! Dog! Pinch and Charley, it's dog!"

It was Mr. John Barrow, running at a pretty good rate even with the weight of that dog-fur blanket under his arm. He slowed down and stopped right in front of Mr. Short.

"Where's Cat Eyes? I'm gonna tell him you cheated us, trading dog for muskrat," Mr. John Barrow yelled.

Mr. Short glared at him. "Then, give the furs back to me." He snatched the blanket from Mr. John Barrow and threw it on the ground.

"You!" He pointed at Billy Sweet. "Haul these rare furs to the boat."

Mr. John Barrow switched from angry to sad.

"Can't I keep it if it ain't worth anything? I worked hard, sewing those hides together." But Billy had already rolled it up and slung it on his shoulder. He was moving toward the bayou.

Mr. Short turned back to me and Charley. His face was red and angry. He grabbed a pitchfork that leaned against the barn wall and stabbed it in our direction. The prongs were as sharp as needles.

"I have reached the limits of my patience in this matter. Young man, you tell me where those poles are hidden this very minute or I'll fill you full of tiny holes and all your blood will drain out and the rats will eat your flesh."

"No you won't," said a voice behind him.

I knew all the time that it would happen. That's

the way it always happens. Right at the very last minute, the hero wins and the villain loses.

It was Cat Eyes, halfway down the stairs to the barn loft. His big pistol was in his hand and leveled on Mr. Short. But that wasn't the best thing. In his other arm he cuddled a little goat, a soft, warm, gray-colored goat just like its momma. I rushed to the foot of the stairs, arms stretched out.

"I'm back in charge now, Pinch. You take hold of your little goat." He handed it to me. I hugged the cute little devil and it started sniffing my nose the minute I had it in my arms. It was skinny, but plenty much alive. Then Cat Eyes gave Henry a nod and Henry went up into the loft and came back down with two more little gray goats and a bunch of empty ninny bottles.

"We ran out of milk, Pinch. I been feeding these little varmints four times a day and I'm sick and tired of doing it." Henry handed them to Charley.

"We got to get warm milk into their bellies," I told Cat Eyes and headed for the door. "Their momma's ready and waiting to feed them this very minute."

"First the poles," Mr. Short said, blocking my way.

"Never mind about the poles," Cat Eyes said. "You won't be needing them in jail."

"But . . ." Mr. Short mumbled.

Cat Eyes lifted up his gun and pointed it at Mr. Short. "I'll handle this," he said. "Pinch, you run on home quick. Tell your paw I got things under control again. He can come get his furs when he's good and ready. And Pinch, while you're gone, why don't you leave John Barrow behind to help me guard these critters. That make sense to you?"

It did. I gave the little goat a kiss and started walking away.

"And, Pinch," Cat Eyes called, "maybe you ought to tell John where the boat poles are hid, just so somebody will know."

I had to get home quick. If the little goats didn't get fed, they would die.

I pulled Mr. John Barrow aside and told him where the boat poles were, not letting anybody else hear. He looked at me and grinned.

Then for a minute I stopped thinking about the little goats and remembered what Cat Eyes had told me about not trusting people.

"Mr. John Barrow, don't you tell a soul, you hear? Not a soul!"

We left Mr. John Barrow and Cat Eyes there, keeping watch.

⊙ 27 ⊙

The Boat Poles

Dad was tying the horse to the wagon when we got back to the store. I told him what had happened.

"If we don't get back there quick, they might get the best of Cat Eyes again and get away with the furs," I said. "Let's go."

We turned the little goats over to Mom. She carried them to where Loretta was tied to a tree, and feeding time started.

"Three kids is a pretty good bunch, Pinch. We are on our way to a genuine goat farm."

The men loaded into the wagon and we started out. We hadn't gone too far down the road when Charley shouted to me.

"Pinch, guess who that is coming across the field?"

It was Mr. John Barrow, just poking along.

"And what you think that is under his arm?"

Somehow he'd gotten the dog-fur blanket back from Mr. Short. That was like him. He was ready to bargain the striped shirt off a jailbird.

"Everything all right back there, Mr. John Barrow?"

"Hi, everybody," he said. "Nice and peaceful at the barn."

"How'd you get the blanket back?"

"Pinch, that little man up and gave it to me." There was a softness to his voice, almost like when he had been talking to his paw.

"Why ain't you keeping watch with that Cat Eyes fellow like you was supposed to?" Mr. Ben Riedlinger asked.

"I got chores, Ben. Besides, the excitement's all over now that everybody's got what's coming to them." He shifted the blanket to his other arm and shuffled off. Dad gave the reins a flip and we started moving again, but when Mr. John Barrow called my name, we stopped and looked back.

He was looking only at me. There was fear in his eyes.

"I didn't do it on purpose, Pinch. He said he would shoot me unless I did it." Then he turned and ran.

I grabbed Dad on the shoulder. "Make this wagon move!" I yelled to him.

It was quiet when we got near the barn. It was quieter still when we got inside. I climbed the stairs to the loft. A rat scurried into a corner. But that rat was the only living thing to be seen. The loft was empty.

Dad and Mr. Ben Riedlinger started running

toward the boat landing. Me and Charley ran even faster.

The flatboat was about a quarter way out into the bayou and moving good. Mr. Short was poling at the stern with the gray people helping. Mrs. Long was poling at the bow. Her flowery hat made her look almost as tall as the pole she was using. She wiped her brow. Then she saw us standing on the bank. She gave a dainty wave.

The water was swift and they were halfway across and into the main current before Charley and I could even start throwing stones. Mr. Short looked up suddenly from his poling. He saw us. He stopped poling and lifted a hand to wave happily. There was a thin, mean smile on his face.

Then he stopped waving and pointed to the very top of the stack of muskrat furs.

Sitting at the highest point, laughing his skinny gray head off, was Cat Eyes O'Toole. His laughter danced across the water, taunting us until the boat disappeared around the turn in the bayou.

◉ 28 ◉

The Letter

It was a hard winter, but nobody starved or went cold. We shared with the Riedlingers and they shared with others. The men did pretty good in the trapping pool.

I helped Mr. Tony at the store whenever I could. Then came the afternoon when I headed for the store to help shelve cans and met Mr. Tony in the middle of the road heading for our house.

"Pretty good news, Pinch," he yelled when he saw me. "They caught those little people, Cat Eyes, the whole bunch. They got them locked up in jail about twenty miles down the bayou. Those scoundrels tried it again and got caught."

"Will we get our muskrat hides back?"

"I think we'll get some of them, son. But not all. Lots of people claimed they got cheated. It's hard proving ownership of a muskrat hide once you turn it loose."

It was better than nothing, but I'd been hoping we'd get everything back that was ours.

"If I'd listened to Cat Eyes when he said not to trust people, things might've been better," I told him. "I never should've told Mr. John Barrow where we hid the poles."

"Son, John told me Cat Eyes would've killed him with that silver gun if he hadn't told."

"I don't think so."

He stomped his foot on the ground so hard he raised a puff of dust.

"Pinch, how you going to live without trust? You got to trust most people most of the time. You trust Charley, even when you and him ain't talking. And you said yourself, John taught you plenty this year about muskrat trapping."

We walked back toward my house and thought our thoughts. At the porch steps he turned to me and smiled.

"I been thinking about how far I would trust Henry and Billy Sweet. You know, I guess you got to draw the line somewheres."

He went inside to talk to Dad. I went looking for Charley. Things just didn't feel finished. Charley and I talked some about it and he felt the same way.

"So, what do we do about it?" I asked him.

Little sparkles came into his eyes.

Early next morning Mr. John Barrow came banging on my front door. He stood on the porch, waving a letter in my face.

"Know what this is, Pinch? It's a letter from that pretty little Mrs. Long, that's what it is." He was grinning and stomping around the porch, too happy to keep still.

"She wants to marry me, Pinch! Lordy, I'd about given up on gitting married."

"Where is she?"

"Only about twenty miles from here. She mailed it from a jailhouse. She is staying there a day or two with a friend who is the jailer. That little lady says she really misses me. Imagine that!

"Says if I'll jist send her twenty dollars care of the jailhouse, she'll be here for the wedding the very next day."

"What you going to do?"

"Couldn't break her heart, Pinch. I sent the money I been saving for my new mule."

At sunup, he was out on the front porch of the store, dressed in his Sunday suit, waiting for his bride. All morning long he jawed happily with anybody who would listen. He asked five different grownups to be best man in the wedding and every one of them turned him down.

Midafternoon, the sky clouded. So did his smile. He sat on the bottom step, picking his teeth with a stick.

About suppertime it began to drizzle. He stood up, stretched his skinny bones and threw the stick away.

I watched from across the road. A cross-eyed mule couldn't look any sorrier than he did.

"Mr. John Barrow?" I called.

He turned and stared, his face wet from the rain.

"It was me and Charley that sent you the letter

from Mrs. Long. We shouldn't have, but we were so darned mad at you about the boat poles."

It took a minute for the words to get inside his thick head. Then, instead of stomping and yelling like I figured he would, he grinned at me like a greedy hound dog and came running up with his hand stretched out.

"Mighty good trick you pulled on me, Pinch! Now gimme back my twenty dollars!"

"Mrs. Long's probably spending it on another flowery hat this very minute," I said, grinning at him. Dad says the worst thing in the world is feeling good after you've done something bad. But I couldn't help myself.

"You mean I ain't going to git my twenty dollars back?"

He dropped his hand to his side and stared prickly thorns at me. Then he whipped around and headed toward home.

About ten yards down the road he twisted around and came walking slowly back. He stopped right in front of me but didn't say a word. He stuck his hands in his pockets, looking all around, eyes squinched against the drizzle.

"Ought to be sweet smelling by tomorrow after all this rain," he said pleasantly.

Then he stopped looking all around. His eyes landed square on me.

"You know what I'm planning to do?"

"What?"

He gave me a crooked smile.

"Wait and see, you little varmint," he said, each word soft and sweet as a dab of honey.

He drew his skinny self up tall, turned around and strutted off, feet squishing the puddles and making the water splash.